MW00533538

GENESIS OF LIGHT

LIGHT AND SHADOW CHRONICLES NOVELLAS
BOOK 1

D. M. CAIN

Published 2021 by Next Chapter

Cover art by Cover Mint

Edited by Pam Elise Harris

Back cover texture by David M. Schrader, used under license
from Shutterstock.com

This book is a work of fiction. Names, characters, places, and incidents are the product of the author's imagination or are used fictitiously. Any resemblance to actual events, locales, or persons, living or dead, is purely coincidental.

ACKNOWLEDGMENTS

Thank you to my wonderful family for all your support. Thank you to Mum who always listens to my radio interviews and shares my posts, Carl who reads my books every time they're released and Dad who always believes in me and supports my dreams.

I couldn't do this without you. Thank you all.

Cover Design, map and family tree by Irina French:
www.irinafrench.com www.
facebook.com/irinafrenchdigitalart
Edited by Pam Elise Harris https://kitchensinkedits.
wordpress.com/
Proofread by Cassandra Metcalfe
https://veritasauthorservices.wordpress.com
Proofread by Indelible Think http://www.indeliblethink.
co.uk/

AUTHOR'S NOTE

The Light and Shadow Chronicles span thousands of years, and each book tells the story of one character in the tale. The books can be read in any order, and characters dip in and out of each novel. One book may tell the story of a man in his adulthood. The next may be set after that character's death or before his birth.

Putting the story together is up to you—the order of events is not important.
But every story leads the different strands of the legend to the same conclusion...
The final battle...
The apocalypse.

For those who have read *A Chronicle of Chaos*:
This story takes place one hundred and thirty-five years before the events of *A Chronicle of Chaos*. Chaos will not be born for one hundred and fifteen years.

For those who have read *The Shield of Soren*:
This story takes place one hundred and one years before Soren Nitaya is born.

CHAPTER ONE

The landscape wasn't beautiful as such. It should have been. All the usual elements of beauty were there—sweeping meadows, flowers bobbing in the gentle breeze and trees standing watch over them, majestic and peaceful. Even the city down below, at the bottom of the hill, looked beautiful on this day, with the sunlight glittering on the windows of office blocks. But Callista saw no joy in the view before her. Not today.

"One year. I can't believe it's been one year already." Callista's voice was barely audible. She clenched her fists, trying to squeeze the pain away, but, however much she squeezed, nothing would bring her parents back. In her hand was the golden necklace her mother had given her as a child. It was beautiful and intricately carved, studded with diamonds in a cross. She turned it over in her hand and tried to picture the day she had received it, but the memories were distant, and the day had blurred together with the ones that followed.

"The first year is the hardest. But it will get better, I promise. You'll miss them like mad. That part will never go away, but you'll find new ways to deal with it, and you'll find yourself thinking about other things more and your parents less."

Callista looked at Tom, who somehow always knew what to say, and felt a grin spread across her lips. She tucked the necklace back inside her shirt to keep it safe.

"Good job I've got you here. I wouldn't want to do this on my own."

Tom gave her a wide smile, and his eyes flashed with genuine warmth. "No problem," he said. "Someone has to look after you, don't they?"

Callista's smile turned into a frown. "I can look after myself, you know. I just meant that it's good having somebody to talk to."

"Yeah, yeah. It's OK to admit you need a man to help." A sly smirk played on Tom's face.

"I don't need a man to look after me! I am more than capable of dealing with whatever comes my way, and you know it."

Tom lay back on the grass, arms behind his head, and laughed hard at Callista. She huffed and crossed her arms. He was deliberately aggravating her, she knew that, but it took her mind off the anniversary of her parents' death and that was precisely what she needed. That was why he did it.

Her eyes drifted to the view before them. Pabell was a small city and her neighbourhood was close-knit and friendly. Many of the residents were people she considered friends. When her parents had passed away, she knew she could have gone to her neighbours for help, but her pride was too strong for that. She had needed to show the world she could cope on her own.

Luckily, she didn't have to get a job. That was one weight off her mind. Her live-in nanny and housekeeper, Yvonne, had been with them for years. She stayed around and took care of

Callista when Karla and Stanley Nienna died. Mood swings, bad behaviour and skipping school, were all frequent issues Yvonne had to contend with. Luckily for Callista, Yvonne had super-human patience dealing with the recently bereaved teenager.

Tom helped her just as much, but Callista would never say that to his face, his rugged, handsome face. Stealing a sneaky glance at Tom, who lay beside her, Callista grinned.

It was Friday again. It was always a Friday when they met. Sometimes it was to practise the martial arts they learned together, sometimes it was just to talk. But it was the highlight of her week and she wouldn't miss it for the world. It didn't matter what they did, just being with Tom was enough.

After all, he was the only person who didn't think she was crazy when she said her parents were murdered. Karla and Stanley Nienna were not, and never had been, involved in the shady underworld of illegal Sarro dealing. To even suggest they had died in a filthy alley due to drug overdoses was ludicrous to Callista. But no matter how many times she said it, nobody believed her, except Tom. Only Tom agreed it didn't add up. Only Tom listened, actually listened, instead of suggesting she was tired or suffering from delusional grief. It was why she had clung to him at first, and why she had continued to cling to him ever since.

The evening was drawing in, the sky just beginning to turn pink as the sun slowly dipped beyond the horizon. It was beautiful. Tom sat up beside her and looked out over the city. "The sky's too red," he muttered, then lay back down again.

"What?" Callista laughed. "Too red? It's beautiful!"

"Nah. Too red," Tom repeated. Callista aimed a playful punch at his shoulder.

"Hey!" he cried out, but his face broke into a smile. They

grinned at one another, and Callista felt her cheeks burn. Tom was the first to tear his eyes away.

The smile dropped from his lips. "It really is too red though, don't you think?"

Callista's heart leapt into her throat as she followed his gaze. This wasn't just a sunset. The sky was blood red throughout, not the scattered, fading patches of pink that usually came with the sun's descent. Something was wrong.

Everything happened in an instant. The sky tore open with a deafening crack and the ground beneath their feet shuddered. A deep boom and then fireballs were shooting through the air and plummeting down to the city. Callista gasped and jumped to her feet. Even from this distance, she swore she could hear the screams of terrified people as the city was obliterated. Buildings were flattened, reduced to smouldering rubble within seconds. It was as if the gods themselves were hurling rocks from the sky, decimating everywhere and everyone she loved. Tears welled in her eyes, her mouth wide with horror.

Between the crumbling buildings and blazing infernos, Callista caught a glimpse of something impossible and unimaginable. She shook her head but when she looked back again it was still there. An enormous creature of towering height, unlike anything she had ever seen before. Engulfed with dripping lava and leaving wafts of sulphuric smoke in its wake, it skulked through the burning city. It swiped indiscriminately with gigantic burning fists, smashing aside buildings and trees, and crushing the bones of any living thing in its path.

Slowly, as if recognising Callista's presence, it turned to look at her. Sizzling eyes of such intense evil focused upon her petrified form. It held her gaze for a moment, then turned away. As quickly as it had emerged, it disappeared behind the remaining buildings and out of sight.

It was as if it had made a choice not to hunt her down, to let her live. She would have been thankful were it not for the sheer terror that locked her feet in place and made her heart thunder.

Smouldering rocks began to pelt down, but thankfully much smaller stones than the ones obliterating the city. Tom pulled Callista into his arms, trying to protect her, but a rock the size of a penny hurtled out of nowhere and struck her on the forehead. Lights erupted in her vision and intense agony seared through her like a red-hot poker pressed to her skin. She cried out as Tom held his hands above them for protection. A rock hit him, sending him reeling away. He clutched at his injured arm as blood ran down to his fingertips.

Hundreds of tiny stones rained down upon them, burning hot, searing their flesh as they hit. The ground lurched, and Callista was thrown off her feet onto the grass. Her head spun and her vision clouded. With aching limbs, she tried to lever herself up from the ground, but an agonising gash in her forearm made her collapse again.

Lying with her face pressed into ash and mud, and with rocks slamming into her prone body, she considered giving up, staying there in the dust to die alongside her family and friends who had probably failed to make it out of the doomed city before it fell. She could see her parents again. Closing her eyes, she allowed a rare moment of peace to drift over her. She blotted out the noise of the dead and dying, the screams of pain and loss. In the distance, buildings fell, crashing with almighty force into heaps of twisted metal and smouldering rock.

The ground began to shake again with violent aftershocks that jolted Callista's bones. She yelped, turning over onto her back as rifts began to wrench the ground apart beneath her.

She was pulled from the churning horror in her stomach by a firm hand grasping hers.

"Get up!"

She peered through the smoky air, thick with the ash and embers of burning buildings and bodies. The voice came again.

"Callista!"

Tom's hand was warm and strong upon hers, and she pulled herself to her blistered feet. When she stood, she saw the reason for his panic. The city was crumbling and falling, hundreds of buildings bursting into splinters of wood and twisted metal. But beyond that, something even more terrifying was coming their way.

Flanking the city was the ocean and it was changing. It was no longer made up of the calm, crystal blue waves Callista surfed and swam in. The waters were frothy and turbulent, splashing and spraying, as if a giant creature beneath the waves was frantically thrashing and trying to rise from the depths.

A deafening boom sent a wave of red-hot air flowing over them, stinging their eyes and singeing their hair. The ground tremored, and the sea was slowly sucked backwards, away from the city and the beach.

"We have to go, now," Tom said.

Out in the ocean, a wave was beginning to form, a monstrous, towering tsunami that grew and grew with every drop of water it swallowed and every metre it advanced. It rushed towards the beach, swelling with more and more water in its wake.

Callista and Tom ran, hand in hand, across the meadows on the outskirts of the city. There were no buildings here, nothing to protect them from the devastating wave and the detritus it would drag along with it.

They ran as fast as they could, pushing their screaming muscles and pounding hearts as the water thundered behind them at astonishing speed.

On the outskirts of the city was a tall hill that Callista and Tom often used for hunting and practising their fighting skills.

"Tom! Barrow's Hill!" Callista cried, and together they veered for their favourite training ground.

They powered up the hill, their calves aching with every stride.

The water was advancing. Callista swore she could feel the cold spray of the deadly water behind her.

When they reached the top of the wooded hill, they collapsed, exhausted, on the ground. Their chests heaved up and down as they gasped in huge breaths that made their lungs burn with the exertion. They had no idea if they would be high enough to avoid the water, but they knew they could go no further. If this wasn't enough, they would die. All they could do was wait.

They lay side by side, their chests heaving and hands locked.

The water crashed towards them, sweeping along everything it touched. Bodies were wrenched from their resting places and smashed to pieces amongst the flowing rubble.

Callista gasped with horror as the water approached. She leaned over and grabbed onto Tom, burying her head in his neck. The tears began to fall, and she whispered a prayer.

She dared to glance up.

The water was just one hundred metres away. The waves crashed, followed by screams wiped out in a split-second as the tsunami hit.

Fifty metres away. Tom's warm arms wrapped around her.

Ten metres. The fear was worse than seeing her approaching death. Callista couldn't help looking up. Barrow's Hill wasn't high enough. The wave would surely strike them.

She let out a yelp of terror, but just before the water enveloped them, the wave seemed to lose its power. The raging tsunami, which only seconds earlier had been a ferocious beast, withered away into nothing. The water spread out into a calm lake, inches from their feet.

Callista wanted to feel relieved, but all she felt was a cold chill running down her spine. The way the water had stopped wasn't natural, it was almost like the wave itself didn't want to harm her. Was the force that started the apocalypse when she was out of the city the same force that had shielded her from falling buildings and fireballs? It felt like she was being protected, and it terrified her.

Tom jumped to his feet and dragged her into his arms, yelling with delight and planting warm kisses on her cheek. She blushed and pushed her friend away. If there was any embarrassment for his actions, it didn't show on his handsome dark features. His grin spread from ear to ear.

"I can't believe it! We survived!"

Callista looked out at the lake that now covered the land they had run through. Pabell was gone. Completely gone. The city in which she had grown up, played and fallen in love in, had gone. She put her hand up to her mouth as tears ran over her fingers.

The tips of buildings were just visible, poking out of the calm water. Pieces of wood and metal floated to the surface, filth and dust giving the water a grey coating. When bloated corpses began to rise to the surface, Callista turned away as choking sobs wracked her body.

CHAPTER TWO

The hill stretched a few miles, then tapered away again to the flatlands that reached all the way across the continent. They dragged their tired limbs to the tip of the mound and looked down across the vastness of the plains.

It took a long time before Callista felt able to talk again. What had happened was so utterly terrifying, that she was having trouble acknowledging it even happened, let alone trying to understand it. If it weren't for Tom's ever-comforting presence at her side, she was sure she would have given up a long time ago. If she had passed into the oblivion of death along with all of her school friends and neighbours, then at least she would have seen her parents again in Heaven, but evidently, fate had a different plan for her. Why had she survived? The unfairness ate at her. Death might be terrifying, but it would have been a brief fear and then release. *This* was fear unlike anything she had ever known. It was all-encompassing, drowning every thought and dwarfing every feeling.

Now she had no choice but to trudge on across an unforgiving landscape, hoping and praying they find respite. But where would they go? What could they be expected to do at a time like this? Stay calm and keep walking towards what was almost certain death? Callista was strong and independent—she always had been—but nothing could have prepared her for this. And the worst thing of all was it made no sense. What had even happened?

With a tentative sideways glance at Tom, she broached the subject. "What do you think happened?"

His jaw tightened. "I don't know. Tectonic plates, natural causes."

"Don't be ridiculous," she said before she paused to chew her lip. "Tom, I saw..." But she couldn't bring herself to mention the hulking creature she had seen stalking through the city. Just the memory made her shudder.

The silence hung between them for a moment before Tom spoke in a hushed voice.

"I saw it too. That thing, whatever it was. I saw it."

Horror crept through Callista's stomach, and she felt bile rise in her throat. "Tom, none of this makes sense. It's all just... wrong. This can't have been a natural disaster."

Tom shrugged his shoulders. "Maybe we imagined that creature."

"Both of us? At the same time?"

"OK, fine. But the fireballs falling from the sky, they were just meteors, right? That kind of thing has happened before. It's not anything unusual."

"Multiple meteors falling all at once in one concentrated area? Sounds unusual to me."

A dark frown crossed his face. "Do you think this was just one city, though?"

"What do you mean?" Her voice was harsher than she had intended.

"Well, what if this happened all over the world? What if every city on the planet has been destroyed?"

A cold shiver ran down Callista's spine. "We don't know that. There's no evidence of that...please don't say that." Her words were a horrified whisper. "If everywhere has been destroyed, then we'll have nowhere to go."

"Where exactly do you think we're going now? Have you got somewhere in mind, or are we just heading into the unknown?"

Through all the shock and fear that had flooded her system, Callista had pushed onwards without giving a second thought to the fact they had nowhere to go. What if they never found another remnant of civilisation? Was this it? Would it be just her and Tom against the world from here on?

"I don't know," she mumbled. "Should we head back and see if anybody survived Pabell? Our friends and families might have..."

"Don't, Callista. Just don't even say that, all right? You know they didn't. If they weren't crushed and burnt by the meteors or the enormous monster, they were drowned, and you know it."

The anger in his voice surprised Callista. She was taken aback momentarily, but one look at his face confirmed her suspicions. He was upset and afraid, and that scared her more than anything else.

"We'll find somewhere else to go then."

"Like where? Got an end-of-the-world bunker you aren't telling me about?"

His sarcastic words reminded her of something she hadn't thought about in a long, long time. "Wait! Tom, I think I know what to do."

He stopped in his tracks and raised one eyebrow.

"Do you remember when I was a kid, and Yvonne used to

make me do those stupid drills? You came on one with us. Do you remember?"

From the bemused look in his eyes, he remembered but apparently didn't think much of them.

"Tom, take this seriously," Callista reprimanded him like a mother scolding her child. "For as long as I can remember, Yvonne made me do those drills where I was supposed to tell her exactly what I'd do if I got separated from her or my parents. She did earthquake drills, flood drills, terrorism drills. They never ended. I got so fed up with them that I didn't take them seriously. At first, it was all just a game to me, but then I got sick of it."

Tom laughed. "I remember. Your parents were so protective of you."

"I don't think it was them doing it. I think it was Yvonne. She seemed obsessed. But she used to tell me what to do and where to go 'if something happened.'"

"Go on then. What did she say to do at the end of the world?"

Callista cast him a reprimanding glare. "She told me to head east because there would always be help to the east."

Tom looked taken aback. "Really? Just 'east'? That's a bit vague. What kind of help is in the east?"

"No idea, but have you got any better suggestions?"

His silence said it all, and they continued to trudge across the desolate plains, every step taking them further away from Pabell and the life they had once known.

To the south was a vast mountain range, the Jardians if Callista's memory served. The huge range was legendary for being virtually impassable unless one possessed a high level of climbing expertise. Callista most certainly did not wish to attempt that route.

The north would eventually give way to the ocean, and the frozen ice lands, which terrified her as much at the Jardians did.

West would take them back to the ruins of Pabell. Callista never wanted to see the gutted remnants of her hometown ever again. So, east was their only option. Maybe her nanny's advice had been wise after all.

"Do you know," Callista started quietly, "I've never left Pabell?"

Tom laughed and looked at her with incredulity. "No way. I can't believe that Little Miss I'm-So-Brave-Nothing-Frightens-Me could have stayed in boring Pabell all her life."

"Laugh it up all you like, Bast," she said, referring to his second name and the nickname by which most of his classmates knew him. "But there was enough in Pabell to keep me happy. I had no reason to leave."

"Didn't you ever want to explore, to travel?"

She shook her head. "Honestly? No, I didn't. I think I would only have wanted to explore if I was empty somehow or missing something. But I had everything I needed right there, Mum and Dad, Yvonne, my friends..." She hesitated then said the word eating at her, "...you."

As soon as it left her lips, she regretted it. Turning away from his curious gaze, she cursed herself, wishing she could take it back. *Friends, only friends*, she told herself. That was the way it had always been with her and Tom, no matter how much she had dreamed otherwise. She caught the slight smirk and couldn't bear the thought that he was mocking her. Desperate to change the subject, Callista drew the conversation back.

"Maybe if we keep heading east, we'll find another town or city."

"Sure. There can't be empty wastelands forever. We'll hit something eventually," he said, but his voice was distant and strained. Callista could have kicked herself for ruining the atmosphere between herself and the only other living person. Back in Pabell she would have loved the chance to get closer to Tom. Friendship had never quite been enough for her, but now she was just grateful to have him at her side, and she wouldn't want to jeopardise that. She made a mental vow never to let her thoughts wander into that territory again.

"Then, let's do it," she said and marched forwards with renewed energy and vigour. "Maybe if we find somewhere, Yvonne will be there. Maybe there'll be more survivors, and we'll find our friends."

Tom said nothing, and Callista continued, allowing her fantasy to flourish. "All our friends might have made it out. Evan and Grace. They'll be there. Maybe Jess and Alfie too." But with each name she uttered, her mood dropped a little. Each name, intended to bolster her faltering spirit, just deepened her sadness. Her words drifted away into a whisper.

Tom looked steadfastly into the distance, and she could tell her words were bothering him too. All she did was irritate him. That had been her modus operandi throughout the last few years.

Their "friendship" had really been nothing of the sort. Callista had used him, and he her, as a means to focus. He gave her a reason to work hard in martial arts classes and at school. Wanting to beat him at everything, she pushed herself harder and harder, merely for the chance to brag when she met him at lunchtimes. They had never been in the same classes. Callista had been placed in all the top classes, pushed to work harder by the teachers who viewed her as intelligent and capable, something she had never understood herself. Tom, however, languished somewhere in the bottom sets where he answered occasional questions and spent most of his time sitting outside a classroom he had been banished from. Callista had mocked him for it. She mocked him for everything and had probably made his life hell. Why would he want to stick by her at all?

They continued in silence for a while before Callista could hold in the anguish no longer. "Why are you coming this way with me? You could go another way if you want."

Tom looked like he'd been slapped. "Don't you want me to come with you?"

"Of course, I do! I mean...if you want to. I just mean... surely you don't want to be stuck out here with me...so if you find somewhere else to go, I'd understand."

His face creased in a mixture of confusion and amusement. "Now I know you're trying to get rid of me."

"No! No, of course I'm not. I don't know what I'd do without you." She blushed immediately. "I just mean that, of course, I want you here, but I don't know why you'd want to stay with me."

He rolled his eyes and heaved a heavy sigh.

Callista kicked herself again for making the atmosphere weird. She put it down to the tension of their situation. After another few moments of awkward silence, he spoke, pulling her out of her self-chastisement.

"I haven't got anywhere else to go, Callista." He looked at his feet as he walked and ignored her imploring glance. "There's nobody now for me. I left my foster parents as soon as I was able to, and I only had a few friends. Really, you're the closest I've got. So, if you'll have me, I'll keep following wherever you go."

Callista answered before she had a chance to think about it. "I'll always have you."

"Good. Then let's keep going. I'm sure we'll hit civilisation soon. We have to. Eventually, we'll meet some people. Yvonne will be there or other survivors at least. We're not alone in this, I just know it."

Callista was sceptical. The calm, bare landscape before them was a change from the hellfire and brimstone they had witnessed for the past few hours, but it filled her with a different kind of dread. There was no shelter from the hot sun or the driving rain. There were no settlements in the immediate area, and that meant little food or water. Callista could hunt but not very well. It would be down to Tom to feed them both. Her heart twanged with remorse as she realised she had left her staff and sword at home.

They began the journey across the wilderness. Before long, exhaustion started to set in. The horror of escaping the city and the tsunami had worn them down. More than anything they needed sleep. The thought of having to sleep out in the open terrified Callista, so they pushed on in the hope of finding somewhere, anywhere, to sleep.

They trudged on, slowly, as the temperature began to drop. Callista flexed her fingers as an icy cold chill numbed her extremities. Tom had fallen quiet, his hands crammed into his pockets as the bitter wind whipped across the empty, open plains, howling like a banshee.

Eventually, Callista spoke. "Do you really think Yvonne managed to get out?" She shivered, and her teeth chattered. "She's strong, right? Smart. She must have escaped before the city fell. She did. I know she did."

"But...we only escaped because we were out of the city when it happened. Yvonne would have been right at the centre."

Callista threw him a ferocious and intimidating glare. "She made it out! I would be able to feel it if she didn't."

Tom looked away, choosing not to debate with her. Callista knew she was probably the most stubborn person he'd ever met. She still remembered the first day she'd seen him at Pabell Martial Arts Academy. It was four years ago. Tom had been going since the age of nine when his foster parents insisted he take up a cathartic activity to release the pent-up anger he had inside of him from his parents' death. At first, Tom used to smash the pads as hard as he could just to release the pain, but after a while, his technique began to improve, and he learnt restraint and composure. By the age of twelve, he picked up his first black belt.

Then Callista joined. She had transferred from another club when her family had moved house, and she was already a second level junior black belt at the age of twelve. Tom was immediately threatened, and Callista had known he disliked her upon sight. In her second lesson with the club, they sparred. He tried everything he could to land a blow on her, but he couldn't get through her defences and couldn't anticipate her strikes. He obviously wasn't used to being beaten. He got more and more frustrated, and his technique became sloppy. She battered him with a brutal counter and knocked him to the ground. When he got over the humiliation, they became close friends.

When Callista's parents were murdered, Tom was the one she clung to for comfort because he was the only one who understood what it was like to be an orphan. She tried to be strong and hold her head high, even when she was hurting inside. It helped that she had Yvonne to account for her. Callista's mum and dad always seemed to be away on business, but she never knew what it was they did. So Callista grew up with Yvonne, a calm, gentle presence who taught her so much about the world, about history and politics. Callista was fiery and confrontational by nature, but Yvonne taught her to be just and fair. Where Callista's parents forced her to undertake training in three different martial arts, Yvonne encouraged her to consider philosophy, religion, and charity work, and study medicine and law. It was not surprising that Callista was closer to Yvonne than she'd ever been to her parents, but it still hit her hard when they died. She'd never known any other family and was an only child, so now Yvonne, Tom and her other friends were all she had left.

Six hours into their journey, when Callista thought she could barely walk another step, they came across a small encampment. It must have belonged to a group of wandering nomads or tradesmen. There were small tents pitched and the remains of a fire which had long since burned out. But there were no people anywhere to be seen. They walked through the small camp, calling out, but nobody came.

When they accepted the camp was abandoned, they took advantage of the shelter and collapsed gratefully onto the bundle of blankets in one of the tents, ignoring the musty smell of disuse.

Callista drifted into sleep almost instantly, her frayed nerves soothed by the gentle caress of Tom's hands as he stroked her golden hair away from her face. Her skin was grimy and streaked with blood and dirt, but her exhaustion was so great she didn't give it a second thought. He was filthy himself, and her last thought before she drifted into sleep was of how handsome he still looked, even when coated in grime.

CHAPTER THREE

After seven hours or more of sleep, Callista awoke groggily. Tom was nowhere to be seen. Her heart leapt into her throat, and she was immediately wide awake. She jumped to her feet, calling frantically for him as she shot out of the tent to find him stoking the fire in the middle of the camp.

She heaved a huge sigh of relief. "You terrified me. I thought you were gone."

"Never," he replied with a smile. "I fashioned a makeshift trap out of an old box I found in the hedges and managed to catch some rabbits. Want some breakfast?"

Callista hadn't realised just how ravenous she was, and her stomach growled as if on command. She sat down beside him and watched as he skinned and roasted the rabbits. The meat tasted more delicious and succulent than anything she had eaten before.

With the freshly cooked meal still warm in their stomachs and contented from the nourishment, they set off again. A few hours or more into their trek, their bodies were reacting on instinct, working on sheer adrenaline, no longer concentrating on the dull landscape they traversed. It was when their attention slipped that it happened.

First came loud shouts of aggression before three men ambushed them from the side of the road. Their voices were strained and desperate as they demanded everything Callista and Tom had. From the look of the men, they were tired and hungry and most likely as terrified as Tom and Callista were.

"Woah," said Tom, holding both hands aloft in a show of surrender. "We don't mean any harm. If these are your lands, we'll move right on. Please just let us pass in peace."

The men repeated their demands, looking nervous and desperate. Both Tom and Callista were ready, their bodies flexed and ready for an imminent attack.

"No," Tom said firmly, his hands balling into fists at his side. "We're just trying to find someplace to go. You don't need to pick a fight. We're no threat to you."

But the madness and desperation in the men's eyes were absolute, and they were not ready to listen to logic. Before Tom had another chance to reason with them, they launched an attack. They ran for Tom and Callista at the same time, brandishing sticks and rocks as weapons. The largest darted for Tom with a rock held high in his hands, bringing it crashing down towards his head with devastating force. Tom was too quick and ducked the blow, countering with a powerful punch to the man's stomach, making him double over in pain. Tom delivered another brutal punch to the side of the man's jaw, and he dropped to the ground. Another man lunged at him, this one more prepared for a fair fight, and they circled each other, fists at the ready. After a brief moment of respectful hesitation, they launched at each other, throwing punches in a flurry of movements. Grappling with one another, they fell to the ground. Tom wrapped his powerful arms around the other man's, delivering punch after punch to the back of his head and shoulders.

Callista might have been concerned for Tom, but she was attacked before she had the chance to worry. The third man, a scrawny youngster of no more than seventeen, threw himself at her, aiming a punch to knock her down. Callista dodged, utilising her sparring skills. Raising her fists in a block, she readied herself, knowing it would be no trouble to fend off an unpractised, starving boy. But when the attack came, it wasn't anything like what she expected. Accustomed to rigid rules, she hadn't been expecting attacks that fell outside of sparring regulations.

He threw punches at her left and right. She managed to knock the majority aside, but the sheer energy behind his attacks surprised her. She was battered painfully and sent reeling before she had time to plan her defence.

Dragging herself back up, she managed to land one hard swing to his jaw.

It didn't keep him down for long though. The man got to his feet and threw himself at her midriff, knocking her down. Callista tried to block with her arms again, but he drove a fist into her lower abdomen, below her belt level, and she crumpled in pain.

She lashed out with a sharp kick and caught his left knee. He shrieked with pain as he fell beside her, but he was far from finished. His hand clamped around her throat and squeezed down on her windpipe with brutal force. Callista lashed out at the man with all of her strength, trying to beat him away with her fists, but nothing she did even slowed him down. There was pleasure in his bloodthirsty eyes, and he licked his lips in excitement as he crushed her windpipe tighter. He was going to kill her, and he was going to enjoy it.

The sight of his demented face would have been the last

thing she saw, but as she started to drift into darkness, something smashed into the man's head, knocking him off her and sending him sprawling to the ground with a bloody gash on the side of his head.

"Stay the hell away from her, or I'll kill you. *I will kill you,*" Tom repeated with a furious hiss as the man staggered to his feet, wiped the trickling blood from his eyes and stumbled away from them.

Callista choked and rubbed at her sore neck to relieve the pressure that had threatened to crush her windpipe. When she tried to speak again, her throat was agonisingly painful.

"Thank you, Tom," she croaked.

"Are you OK?" he asked, tilting her chin up so he could get a look at her neck. "You'll have some bruising there, but it doesn't look like he did any more damage than that."

She felt like she could cry, and she clung with both hands to his fingers that rested just below her chin. He clutched her hand, offering comfort. "I don't...I don't understand. We're all just trying to survive. Why would they do that to us?"

"It's every man for himself now. Are you OK?"

She hesitated. "Yes...no...I don't know. I don't know why I..." Her words drifted away into silence, and she found herself gritting her teeth. "I don't know why I couldn't fight him off. I've sparred hundreds of times, Tom. I've won medals and trophies. One of the best, that's what the sensei said. How come I couldn't fight off some dumb kid?"

Tom sighed with a handsome frown. "Because you haven't really learnt to fight."

"Yes, I have. I fight all the time. I've fought you. I know how to fight."

"No, you don't. You know how to spar. It's completely different. In sparring, there are rules and regulations. It's fair and orderly, and there is a referee. Fighting for survival is totally different. It's wild and dirty. There are no rules. The only aim is to hurt the other person. No chivalry or honour. Just pure aggression."

Callista couldn't help her face screwing up into an angry frown. "I was one of the best."

"I know, Callista. You beat me at sparring enough times. But that guy didn't care how well you knew the stances and techniques, did he? He just wanted to hit you. You can spar, but you don't know how to fight. I'm not blaming you. It isn't your fault. You've never had to fight properly before."

"And you have?" she snapped, feeling embarrassed to have been beaten in front of Tom.

"Yes, I have," he replied. "I've been in so many fights you wouldn't believe it. Fights at school, fights on the streets with my foster brothers. I've been beaten up and left for dead numerous times. I've learnt a lot."

She stared at him with disbelieving eyes. "You were beaten up?"

He grinned, and she was suddenly aware that she still had a hold on his fingers. She quickly let go. "Don't feel sorry for me, Callista," he said. "It toughened me up. It was exactly what I needed."

Callista doubted that was really the way for him to be brought up, but she said nothing. Tom's background had been a subject of contention for a long time. She never failed to be surprised at how decently he had turned out, considering his sad and unstable past.

"Tom, will you teach me how to fight? Street fight, I mean?"

That grin again. "You want me to teach you how to fight dirty? You're on."

For the next few hours, Tom taught Callista all the moves he had learnt on the street—how to get out of holds and grabs, how to wrestle people to the ground and how to do counter-attacks that didn't fall under the list of "accepted strikes." It didn't take long for Callista to pick up the basics, and she began to feel more confident under his tuition.

Sweating profusely, and both smiling after the exertion, they rested a while, then headed onwards.

CHAPTER FOUR

Along the way, they stopped and practised the moves whenever they could, but the fun and excitement of learning something new was beginning to wear off for Callista. Even the thrill of having Tom so close to her as he demonstrated moves was failing to give her the buzz it had hours ago and the weary drag of the long journey started to pull at her again.

Callista began to fear that these desolate plains would be the last thing she would ever see. She turned to look at Tom. His handsome, dark features looked drawn and tired. His cheeks were gaunt, his skin sallow. His listless eyes had lost their mischievous vigour. Seeing what this was doing to him depressed her further, so she turned forwards again.

The trail they followed never seemed to end. It was a winding path to nowhere. At least, that was how it felt to Callista. Every step she took dragged at her energy, and she staggered on until she felt like she could barely move.

"I can't," she said in a breathless gasp. "Tom, I can't do this anymore."

"Come on, Cal. We can't stop here, can we?" He waved his

arms to indicate the barren landscape all around them. "I know you're tired, but we need to push on until we find something."

Shaking her head in defiance, like a toddler having a tantrum, she glared at him. "No, Tom. I can't. I'm so tired. What are we even doing this for? There'll be nothing there, and you know it. The world is finished. What's the point of anything anymore? Everything we knew, everybody we knew, is gone. Forever."

"You don't know that. Neither of us will know what the future holds unless we keep on and find some other survivors who can tell us what the hell has happened."

A sad shake of her head and Callista felt the vigour and determination drain from her. "If we are going to keep ourselves alive, we can't burn out. We'll need our energy over the coming days and weeks, months or years even. Please, let's just stop and camp here. You managed to catch food before." Exhaustion pulled her down to the ground where she collapsed into a heap, head bowed.

"No," Tom replied firmly, dropping to his haunches beside her and grasping her shoulders. "We can't keep going that way. It was a fluke we managed to fight off those guys on the road. What if more come, huh? How will you be able to fight them in your current state? And look at the terrain here. There isn't a bush or tree for miles. What animals do you expect me to catch exactly?"

Callista felt like crying. A painful lump grew at the back of her throat, and she swallowed it back down, bringing tears to her eyes. Why did she have to survive? In this desolate new world, the dead had at least been given the mercy of a quick death. They had avoided the inevitable horror of the aftermath: the starvation, people turning upon each other and the knowledge that they were the last people alive. Yes, she was quite sure that the dead were the lucky ones.

"I can't."

"Don't say that, Callista! You can! I know you, and I know your strength. If anybody can do this, it's you. Now get up, and let's keep on to this safe point."

"It's not that I can't. It's that...I don't want to do this. What's the point? What kind of future is there for us now? I just want to...to let it win. I want to give up, Tom."

"You can't give up! Imagine if I'd given up when my mum and dad died? Or if my foster parents had given up on me when I was being a nightmare? They knew what had to be done, and they pushed me towards the only thing that enabled me to heal, kickboxing. Just like I'm doing to you now. I'm not letting you give up, even though you're being a pain in the ass. I'm pushing you towards this meeting point because it's the only thing that will make you heal. Now stop being so melodramatic and pick yourself up."

She was staring at him with wide eyes, surprised by his outburst. "I don't think I..."

"Don't you dare say you can't! You can. I know because I've seen you smile through hours upon hours of gruelling training, and more than all of that, I've seen you live through the death of both of your parents and still emerge with your head high. So don't you dare tell me that Callista Nienna is going to die on a dreary field because she couldn't be bothered to fight anymore."

Inspired by his words, and more than a little ashamed of herself, she took his outstretched hand and allowed him to pull her to her aching feet. Blisters stung her heels, and every muscle in her calves and thighs screamed with the discomfort of supporting her weight again. But there was a new energy inside her, a remnant of determination that she hadn't realised was still there. Taking the first step was the hardest, but then she fell back into the rhythm, bolstered by Tom by her side.

She didn't know how many more hours they walked. After

a while, her pain faded to a dull ache, now accustomed to the discomfort she forced upon her exhausted body.

"Callista!" Tom stopped her, placing a hand on her shoulder. "What's that over there?"

Across the empty wasteland on the horizon, they could just make out the remains of a town. It must've been half a kilometre away, but even from this distance they could see the crumbling, destroyed buildings and columns of smoke rising high into the air. They stopped and stared in silence for a few moments.

"I think...," Tom said, "I think it's the safe point."

"Do you think it's OK to go over?" Callista asked.

"I don't know. Maybe it's just ruined, and everybody there is dead."

Callista shuddered. These past two days she'd seen enough death to last her a lifetime. "But maybe there will be food, shelter or medical supplies."

"Yeah, and maybe there'll be fiercely territorial survivors guarding it," Tom rationalised.

Callista frowned. "Maybe they need our help. What if there are injured people or orphaned kids?"

Tom cast her a wry smile. "You can convince me of anything. Come on then. Let's go and see."

They made their way across the open land, keeping their senses alert, but only ruins crept into clear view. Callista was secretly relieved they had found something, anything. The desolate oblivion of the featureless paths was beginning to wear at her body and mind. She felt like her sanity was being stretched to breaking point.

It took them another hour to make the journey to the camp and by the time they approached, both Callista and Tom were exhausted and filthy. Their hair was coarse and riddled with dirt. Callista's was no longer a bright golden blonde. Instead, it had turned a dull sandy colour and Tom's thick black hair was mottled with sandy grains. Callista glanced at him through exhausted eyes. He looked tired and weak—weaker than she'd ever seen him —but his features were still stunning.

He caught her staring at him and flashed a cheeky smile. She couldn't help blushing at being caught so obviously checking him out, but it felt so good to see a glimpse of the smile she'd grown up with shining through the dirt and despair. The sight of her blushing made him grin even more, and a devilish look flashed across his eyes as he reached out and took her hand. Her heart was pounding in her chest as his warm fingers grasped hers.

The decimated town loomed before them. Smoking ruins and piles of rubble lay scattered around what was once a small town before the fire had fallen from the sky. They were inland, so they had been safe from the waves, but the smouldering meteors had clearly struck. A few still lay around, burning an orange-red, smelling of tar, the size of wagons.

A few bodies were lying on the ground, contorted, burned and missing parts, but many of them had been dragged into heaps on the outskirts of town. No time for proper burials and too few were left alive to carry them out. A thin but steady column of smoke rose into the air from the centre of the town.

Callista and Tom walked the ruined streets, trying not to look at the destroyed family homes, precious memories burnt to a crisp. They turned a corner to see a central area, what must have been a marketplace or something similar. A fire burned in the centre and around it sat forty to fifty people in varying states. There were dirty, injured people, being treated for various cuts and bruises. A few children ran back and forth, trying to gather anything that could be of use to their haggard, distressed parents. There were angry, determined faces and the tear-streaked devastated features of those who had lost everything.

Callista craned her neck, desperately searching for Yvonne or any of her friends. Each face she looked into was desperate, and the people stared at her, hoping she was one of their missing loved ones.

Huddled at the back of the ragtag bunch of refugees was a middle-aged man, wrapped in filthy grey clothes that might have been brightly coloured at one time. His thinning hair was flyaway and knotted, hanging limply to his head. What unnerved Callista the most was the rhythmic way he rocked backwards and forwards, clutching a jagged piece of white wood with both hands as if his life depended on it.

"I told them," he mumbled, wide-eyed but without any recognition of Callista standing before him. "I tried to warn them all, but they wouldn't listen. They wouldn't listen. They wouldn't listen."

His words blurred into a mumble, timed perfectly with each back and forth rock of his huddled body. In the events of the day, when the fire had fallen, and the world had been destroyed, this man had not just lost his possessions and family, but evidently his mind as well.

As Callista reluctantly left the man to his psychotic rocking, his words changed. "Big creatures. So big. Fire and brimstone. Big, so big." Back to a barely audible murmur and then, "I saw them!" He shouted so loud it made Callista jolt back in surprise, but by the time she turned to look at him, the man had resumed his rocking and the repeated muttering of, "They wouldn't listen. They wouldn't listen."

Suppressing a shudder, Callista continued through the camp with Tom until they reached the central area where multiple tents had been erected.

There was a makeshift medical tent with a hastily painted

green cross upon it. People scurried in and out, carrying bandages and bowls of pain-killing herbs. Callista stared at them numbly, wondering how many medical supplies these people had been able to find and how long they would last. As they approached, a woman in a white apron with a long blonde ponytail hurried out, looking flustered.

"Yvonne!" Callista yelled and threw herself into her nanny's arms.

Yvonne gasped in surprise and dropped the blood-soaked towel she had been carrying. She wrapped her arms around Callista and squeezed her tightly, planting kisses on the top of her head. Callista began to tremble as big wet tears rolled down her cheeks.

Tom stood back, unsure where to look. He crossed his arms and tapped his foot, but Callista knew that look in his eyes. He was feeling uncomfortable rather than impatient. She would have helped him search the survivors for his friends and family, but she knew there was nobody there for him. He'd moved out of his foster parents' house when he reached sixteen, and they had moved away. He didn't even have contact details for them. As for friends, he had never been bothered with them much. Not like Callista. She couldn't face the thought of not having her friends around her.

Callista and Yvonne eventually pulled apart. Yvonne held her at arms' length with tears in her blue eyes. She smiled, full of joy.

"Yvonne, what's happening here? Did you see what happened at Pabell? It's gone, all gone."

Yvonne's eyes glazed over as she answered in a strangely detached voice. "I know, Callista. I know what happened there."

"Where were you when it...?"

Yvonne interrupted her by grasping her shoulders and

looking intently at her face. "I thought you'd died in the city. How did you get out alive?"

"I wasn't in the city when...whatever it was, happened. Tom and I were out in the fields. Otherwise, we would have been dead too."

Yvonne nodded to Tom. "Thank you for taking care of her, Tom."

Tom nodded in response but cast Callista a tiny smirk, a grin that only she recognised. Callista picked it up immediately. It was part of a private joke they'd shared since childhood.

"I can take care of myself. I just brought him along with me," Callista said, knowing Tom was pretending not to hear her.

"That's OK, Yvonne," said Tom, "I couldn't leave her out there in the wilderness. Poor little thing wouldn't know what to do with herself. It's a good thing I was there."

Callista cast him a furious glare. "How dare you? Who hit black belt first? Me or you, huh?" She had her hands on her hips, her eyebrows raised, accusing him.

Tom smirked. "It isn't a competition, sweetheart. Besides, your black belt didn't help you when you were sulking back there, did it?"

She narrowed her green eyes. "I really hate you sometimes, you know that, right?"

"I'm sorry to interrupt whatever's going on here," said Yvonne, waving her hand between Callista and Tom, "but I need help in here before we can catch up. Would you?"

They followed her into the tent and were dismayed to see twenty injured people, lying on blankets spread across the floors. Burns, cuts, even a few missing limbs. It smelt of death and blood, and the injured were in pain. Callista's jaw hit the floor as she reached for Tom's hand. He stroked her trembling fingers.

They didn't have long to gawp as towels, blankets and bandages were thrust at them, and they were thrown into helping out. For the next few hours, they dashed back and forth trying to help the victims. They patched up minor wounds and sent people on their way, to make room for the steady stream of new people being taken in every hour. After a few hours, the trickle of new refugees and survivors slowed. The town, or whatever was left of it, now sheltered nearly two hundred survivors of all ages and backgrounds, but nobody else that Callista, Tom or Yvonne knew. With a heavy heart, Callista began to accept that everybody she had known was gone, and she would never see them again. Whenever that horrifying thought flitted through her mind, she would glance at Tom and feel her heart fill with appreciation that she still had him.

She still had Tom and Yvonne, and she couldn't have asked for much more.

CHAPTER FIVE

As the evening sneaked up on them and the light began to dim, Callista and Tom collapsed, exhausted, by the fire. Six people had died under their care that afternoon, and Callista was pale and quiet. The shock and horror of their deaths dug into her heart and clawed away at her stomach so that when she was offered food, she couldn't face it. Tom ravenously gobbled his portion, and though he made eyes at her untouched meal, he left it for her in case she changed her mind.

There were so many questions rattling around inside Callista's head. She was desperate for some answers because despite how unlikely it might have seemed, Yvonne appeared to know more about this than she was letting on, but Callista was too exhausted to chase it up and argue. Now, she needed rest more than she needed peace of mind.

She tucked her knees up beneath her and rested her head on Tom's shoulder as he ate. He put his plate on the ground and stroked her hair gently. Callista nuzzled into his caress and turned her face to look up at his dark features. Tears were welling in the corners of her eyes, but she wouldn't let them fall. There was something else besides sadness and fear in her, something deeper, stronger. It was a solid determination that burned like fire. Tom smiled and leaned down to place a kiss on her forehead.

She blushed and pulled back for a moment before a smile crept across her lips. With one hand she reached up and pulled him towards her, planting a long, lingering kiss on his mouth. Her whole body tingled as she ran her fingers through his thick, dark hair. It was a fervent, desperate kiss, a plea for safety and security in their ruined world. She needed him now more than ever, and he responded with passion, giving her everything she wanted. When she finally pulled away from him, there was warmth and compassion in his eyes.

As the evening drew to a close, the sun dipped below the horizon, casting their encampment into darkness, save for the fire which burned brightly in the centre. The two hundred survivors huddled around the fire's warmth, some quiet and introspective, some still crying quietly to themselves. When Callista looked around the circle, she saw fear and despair, but she also saw anger brewing in the eyes of the desperate souls who had lost everything.

She had waited long enough for answers. She needed to know what was happening, and she needed to know now.

Prying herself out of Tom's warm arms, Callista made her way over to Yvonne, who was crouched near the fire, stoking the embers with a long stick.

"Yvonne," Callista said quietly, not wanting others to hear their conversation, "What the hell was that in the city? Surely, some scientists or whoever must have detected something and been able to give some warning? Those meteors that fell from the sky...didn't anybody see them coming? Why didn't anyone order an evacuation?"

Yvonne said nothing but kept her eyes on the fire and

continued to stoke the burning logs. Eventually, sighing deeply, she turned to Callista with sadness in her eyes.

"They didn't know, Callista. There was no warning because nobody had any idea it was coming."

"No idea at all? How is that even possible? Someone must have known something."

Yvonne was quiet again, and she avoided Callista's gaze.

"Why are you ignoring me, Yvonne? Yvonne?" she pressed but got no response. "If you don't know, that's fine, but don't damn well ignore me," she muttered and sat back with her knees pulled up to her chest.

Yvonne sighed again, and her intense blue eyes flicked up to her young charge. "Callista," she whispered, "the scientists didn't know, but I did."

Callista stared at her blankly. "What? Don't be silly. How could you know when nobody else did?"

Yvonne looked away again and poked at the fire, more violently this time. Burning logs from the fire crumbled under her aggressive stoking as the flickering embers rose in a flurry of burning lights. Callista waited for an answer, her mind racing. Ever since she was a young child, Yvonne had made Callista run through all the meeting points across the country. She remembered Yvonne dragging her out across the countryside for miles, showing her where a good place would be to hide if "anything ever happened."

"Oh my God," Callista muttered. "You *did* know. You knew all along this was going to happen, didn't you?" Callista's voice got gradually louder as a few people around the fire looked up.

"Keep your voice down," Yvonne hissed. Her eyes flashed Callista a stern warning.

"How did you know?" Callista snapped as Tom appeared

at her side, his arms crossed over his broad chest. "Why didn't you tell somebody?"

Yvonne held her hands out in front of her. "You don't understand! There is nothing I could have done. *Nothing*. I promise you. I knew something was coming, but I didn't know when or where or how it would happen."

Callista scoffed in annoyance. "You did know. You spent my whole life taking me to hiding places in case this happened. That's how I knew to come here! You led me here!"

"Yes, I did, Callista. Because it was important you survived," Yvonne pleaded.

"It was important that everybody survived! But you didn't save them!" Callista's hands curled into fists by her side. "Do you know how many people must have died in the cities? How many of my friends? Look at all these people." She gestured back to the clearing. "All of them have lost their friends and family. Couldn't you have told everybody and saved them all?"

Yvonne shook her head, and her eyes flashed with something that Callista didn't like. There seemed to be little compassion for the people who had died.

"No, Callista, I couldn't. I couldn't risk worldwide panic. If everybody knew the safe places to hide, they would have been swamped. I needed you to survive. *You*, Callista. You don't know it yet, but all this was about you. It was essential that *you* survived the end of civilisation."

"Why me? Why am I so important?"

"Callista, please," she said quietly. "I didn't want it to happen this way, but I *must* talk to you. Please, *please*, calm down and listen to me."

Callista's eyes blurred with tears as Tom placed a reassuring hand on her back. The feel of his touch calmed her nerves a little. "Why should I?" she hissed, bitterly.

"Because," Yvonne hesitated, "Because it's to do with your parents' death. And your destiny."

Callista stared at Yvonne, her heart pounding. How could this have anything to do with her parents? They died a year ago. But there was a nagging deep in the pit of her stomach. The remnant of a distant memory, something she had repressed a long time ago.

It came back to her in hazy flashes.

Callista, as a tiny child, was saying goodbye to her mother and father as they set off on one of their many business trips abroad. She had cried and stamped her little feet, begging them not to leave her at home with Yvonne again. Yvonne had put her hands on Callista's shoulders, trying to calm her down, but Callista had broken free and screamed at her parents. "You're always leaving me! Why are you always leaving me?"

Her mother had knelt before her, taken Callista's hands in hers and looked into her eyes. "You're too little to understand now, but when you're older, we'll tell you. We'll tell you everything."

"I'm not little!"

Her mother smiled and wiped away her tears. "You're right, sweetheart. You're not a baby. But you're still too young to know what awaits you and what a burden we carry in our family. I can't put that on your shoulders yet. Here, take this necklace. Yvonne will help you to look after it and keep it safe. It is special, and one day you will learn why. Keep training, keep learning, and when you are old enough, I promise that you will learn everything."

Callista had thrown herself to the floor, flailing her legs and arms out in every direction. The golden necklace was flung aside, dismissed and Callista shrieked at the top of her voice as her parents cast apologetic glances to Yvonne and stepped out of the front door.

Callista's eyes widened as the memory came back to her. She pulled the golden necklace from her shirt and stared at the stunning gold and diamond jewellery. Looking up at the imploring, genuine expression on Yvonne's face, her heart leapt. Yvonne was right. This was something to do with her. She just knew it.

"OK, tell me everything."

"I can't. I have to show you."

Callista frowned. "Show me what?"

"There's somewhere I have to take you. It'll take at least two days on foot. It's a long way from here."

Callista stared at her, blinking. "What about everybody else? Do we all go?"

"No." The answer was firm and absolute. "Just you."

Tom stepped up beside Callista, his shoulder brushing against hers. "Wherever Callista goes, I go. Especially now. We don't know what the state of the world is. It might be dangerous out there."

Yvonne gave a slight smile, half proud of him for his bravery, half patronising. "Sorry, Tom. But this is for Callista's eyes only. Don't worry. She is more than capable of looking after herself."

"She's right. I am," Callista said, grinning. But the smirk was quickly wiped off her face as she realised she didn't want to go anywhere without him. "But no, Yvonne. I'm not going without Tom."

There was a flash of darkness in Yvonne's expression. Anger, disappointment; Callista couldn't tell, but she didn't argue.

"Fine, but he's your responsibility."

"He always is."

CHAPTER SIX

It was the longest journey Callista had taken in her life. Two days of continuous walking across the wastelands and rolling fields of an unknown land. She had no idea where they were or what this place had once been. There were destroyed settlements dotted on the horizon as they passed, blackened with the ghosts of fires.

There might have been the hope of coming across further signs of civilisation, a town or a city perhaps, if it hadn't been for the fact that the northern part of this country was a desolate wasteland even before the fires came. It was one of the reasons why Callista never strayed beyond the borders of Pabell.

Nothing dotted the horizon or littered their path. It was an open desert, a rolling eternity of nothingness. Desolation.

Before long, Callista, Tom and Yvonne began to pass contorted bodies, which were starting to decay in the warm sun. The horror that Callista first felt upon seeing the dead was beginning to fade, and she was sickened at the realisation that it was becoming normal to her.

They made camp whenever they could, stopping to regain

their energy and to nibble on the meagre supplies they had brought along. They were often so exhausted from the miles they walked that they slipped into a deep sleep as soon as they stopped. Whenever they could stay awake, Callista grilled Yvonne for details, but she refused to tell her anything until they arrived. Where they were going and what they would find when they got there, Yvonne wouldn't say. After a while, Callista stopped asking.

When they arrived, Callista barely noticed. It was Tom gently tugging at her arm and leading her to a bench that made her aware they had reached their destination. Her shaking knees buckled. She collapsed onto the rickety seating, her eyes closed as she cast her face up to the approaching evening sky. The heat of the late afternoon still bore down upon her skin, but she felt none of its comfort. She felt nothing, just a dull numbness that masked her existence, like a bubble had been inflated around her.

Yvonne scurried around, somehow full of energy despite their journey, making food and fetching water to drink. She knelt before Callista and tilted her head back to accept some water. The cool liquid trickled across Callista's cracked, dry lips, and she licked thirstily at the droplets. Yvonne fed her some soup next, a tasty broth she had somehow boiled together from a variety of plants and herbs she had either brought along or found dotted amongst the wasteland plains. Callista slurped her soup with relish, the sustenance revitalising her.

Slowly, comprehension filtered through Callista's addled thoughts. She opened her eyes to look around and gasped. Ancient grey stone walls stood before them, as tall as her old house in Pabell. With the evening sun setting in the sky, the light was dim, and their campfire cast shadows across the walls, shadows that danced with every flicker of flame. Callista held her hand out, and the shadows of her fingers were cast, immense, on the walls surrounding them.

"Woah," Tom murmured, his eyes cast up to the towering ancient wall.

Callista staggered weakly to her feet, stumbling over her heavy, tired limbs, as she shook the numbness from her catatonic muscles. She joined Tom and stared, open-mouthed, at the walls from left to right and realised they had appeared out of nowhere. For miles, nothing had broken the empty desolation and then suddenly these walls sprang up from the dust. Surely, they must have been visible for miles. How come they weren't famous? A tourist attraction perhaps, visited by thousands of history lovers every year?

As if reading her thoughts, Yvonne smiled and stood by Callista's side. "It isn't as easy to find as you would think. You have to know exactly how to navigate to this place. The emptiness of the plains is disorientating. Without a compass, even maps lead people in the wrong direction."

"What's beyond the walls?" Callista asked, still staring dumbfounded.

"Let's go and see." Yvonne started to walk the perimeter of the wall, keeping close to the rock, stepping over and around the fallen piles of rubble.

"Wait! What about our camp?" Callista called, tripping over the loose stones and getting her foot caught in trailing vines.

Yvonne skipped gracefully over the rubble. "We leave it. We'll be back soon anyway, and there's nobody else about."

"But we don't know how long this wall is. What if it takes us days to find a way in?"

Yvonne laughed in a tone far too mocking for Callista's liking. "You're forgetting I know the way in. It isn't far. Come on. It's just up here."

Callista and Tom followed, struggling to keep up with Yvonne's light-footedness. After what felt like an eternity, Yvonne stopped abruptly by a section of wall that looked exactly the same as the previous mile or more.

"Here," she said confidently.

Callista screwed her nose up. "What? How do we get in? I can't see a tunnel or door or path or anything."

Yvonne grinned and gestured with one finger for Callista to step closer. As Callista walked towards Yvonne, the walls seemed to open up before her to reveal a thin crack running between two cliffs made by the walls. Callista gasped. She stepped forwards, and the crack widened. She took a step backwards, and the rocks appeared to merge again, masking the entrance.

"That is so cool," Tom murmured, stepping forwards and backwards, time and time again. "How did you find this?"

"I know lots of things. This passageway is a natural rock formation that an ancient civilisation used to their advantage when building their city. They used nature to conceal what they had made."

Excitement bubbled in the pit of Callista's stomach, and her exhaustion and despondency were momentarily forgotten. "So, the biggest question is, what's inside that they needed to hide so carefully?"

"Want to find out?"

"Absolutely."

Yvonne led the way, ducking through into the narrow passageway between the rock faces. Callista followed, placing her hands on either side to steady her descent into the depths of the unknown enclosure. They passed along a hundred metres or more of the winding path, with Callista staring up at the immense fracture. She surmised it must have been caused by an earthquake or by millions of years of steady erosion, like the monumental canyons she had seen in pictures.

The passage began to widen and the view opened up into a sweeping vista that took Callista's breath away. Stretching for miles before her was a landscape of ruins, ancient crumbling buildings scattered with rubble and with trailing moss and ivy snaking jagged lines across the stonework.

Callista wandered in, amazed, and nearly tripped over a fragment of rock. She bent to pick it up and inspected it carefully, running her fingers over the grooves. Nearby, a column caught her eye, an immense plinth that could once have held up a building. Callista held up the shard of stone and saw it fit into the column. It reminded her of places she had studied as a child, sunny islands with vivid azure oceans and sparkling white houses dotted along the coast. And towering above the picturesque villages were the enormous remains of architecture from ages past.

She glanced around, her eyes falling upon a whole range of incredible buildings, colonnaded temples with domed roofs, and intricately carved sculptures. There were dried up, moss-covered fountains, and a wide-open courtyard. And around it all were the imposing stone walls made of the natural cliff face, obscuring these treasures from the world.

Callista felt like a child again as she skipped around the ruins, staring with wonder at the ancient text and pictures carved into the stone. Jumping gleefully over fallen columns, she laughed and spun on the spot, taking in the sight.

Tom watched Callista fondly. "She's just a big kid really," he said to Yvonne.

"She can't be a kid for much longer. The world's a different place now, and she'll have to toughen up to survive."

"I know, and she knows. But for now, just let her enjoy this.

If her carefree nature is going to get quashed out of her, she deserves one last chance to let herself go a bit."

Callista continued to prance around the ruins, pretending not to have heard the words that worried and frightened her, words that proclaimed her childhood was over.

Yvonne called her over to sit on a row of fallen columns.

Callista's eyes widened as she stared up at the delicately carved friezes and statues adorning the apex of the building. They sat down as Yvonne perched on a fallen column opposite them.

"What is this place?" Tom asked.

"Yeah, it's amazing. How come I've never heard of it? Do tourists come here?" Callista added.

"No, Callista. As you saw, it's hidden from the world, and it's hidden for a reason. There are very important and potentially dangerous things here."

Yvonne took a deep breath and leaned in. "This city is ancient. Eight hundred years ago, it was inhabited by a civilisation of powerful warriors. These people were engaged in a brutal and vicious war that raged for centuries. Eventually, the conflict spread to include the whole world. One army was based here. This was the epicentre of their greatness. They called it Alexiria, and it's thought to be one of the oldest and greatest cities humanity ever built. They say the temples stretched into the clouds and silver flags flew from every turret. An ingenious pulley system lifted water up to houses nestled in the sky. To lay eyes upon Alexiria was said to be like witnessing Heaven itself."

Callista and Tom stared, their eyes flitting over the stunning relics and architectural wonders.

Yvonne continued, "The entire world was dragged into the war. Every country, city and town was forced to side with one army or the other. The army based here, at Alexiria, believed in ensuring the protection and well-being of every person in the world. They followed the ways of light and goodness, so they were known as the Children of Light. Their enemy, however, lived in darkness and believed in ambition and power. They called themselves the Brotherhood of Shadow."

Callista, listened, fascinated, and drank in every detail Yvonne shared. "What happened? Did they fight it out?"

"Oh yes," Yvonne said with a sad smile. "When the two armies reached the height of their power, they met in cataclysmic Armageddon. And it wasn't just humans either. Great and powerful creatures with mind-boggling powers stalked through the battlefields, batting aside humans like they were grunts. People with the ability to summon elements and control monsters raged and battled, their terrible powers clashing." Yvonne stopped and pointed to the apex of the building before them where there were carved images of humans alongside angels, demons and monsters. "Both sides of the war had them —magicians, sorcerers, whatever you want to call them—and when their magical powers collided the results were catastrophic. Legend states that the battle was long and bloody. Tens of thousands died."

Tom was as engrossed as Callista. "Who won?"

"Nobody knows. The records are very sparse regarding that part, but it has been speculated that when the war ended, it took everybody out with it. Neither side won, and nothing but ruins remained. There must have been pockets of civilisation that survived, small villages that avoided the conflict and the death, or else humanity could not have survived."

Callista's eyes widened. "Like now. The world is destroyed, and only a few people are left alive. It's just like us now."

"Yes, and humanity survived, did it not?"

Yvonne leant in closer to Callista and continued. "I'd say that ninety percent of the world's population died the first time the world fell. The creatures that stalked the land and caused chaos were gone and have never been seen since."

Callista gasped out loud, interrupting Yvonne's story. "Creatures causing chaos? I saw an enormous, fiery monster in the city. It destroyed everything in its path. We thought maybe we'd just imagined it, didn't we?" She turned to Tom who nodded.

Yvonne shook her head sadly. "Unfortunately not, Callista. Those monsters came the first time the world was destroyed, and they've come again. It is yet another sign that history is repeating itself. The powers those special people from before wielded were destroyed or lost, and no human born since can do such things. After it all ended, a new age was born. This is our age, where life is simple, battles are confined to countries, evil and good are balanced, and people are just...ordinary. But underneath the normality, something was always brewing, stirring. Something or someone wanted the war to begin again and this time for it to truly be resolved."

"But how can it? All the people who fought in the first war have been dead for thousands of years," Tom said.

"Yes, but some of their ideals and their teachings have survived, as you shall see. They say every settlement and every survivor will be pulled into the war again."

"There have been wars before that have involved countries across the world. Like that?" Callista asked.

"No. That was different. That was many countries with many leaders working together and fighting a variety of battles, a variety of disagreements and vendettas. This would be different. The entire world united under one of two leaders. Every nation on the planet following one of these two great warriors until they are potentially strong enough to meet again in Armageddon."

"That's not how it works, though," Callista said. "There

isn't a leader of the entire planet. There are just small groups, small countries, that follow their own leaders."

"There are at the moment, or at least there were just a day or two ago," Yvonne said, casting Callista a meaningful glance. "But the world has changed, hasn't it? Those countries, those leaders, they no longer exist. What if all this destruction was engineered by somebody hoping to pull the remaining survivors together into two armies ready to reignite this ancient war?"

"That's quite a stretch of the imagination. I mean, why would anybody want that? Who would do something so atrocious?"

Yvonne shrugged her shoulders. "A higher being? Or a more corrupt one? Call it what you will, but somebody or something wants a war."

Callista glanced at Tom. It looked like he shared her scepticism. "I don't know, Yvonne. I understand what you're saying about the old legends, and it would make a great story, but a war? Really? What makes you so sure?"

Yvonne's usually calm voice had an edge of hostility. "It shall all become clear soon, and your doubts will be silenced, I assure you."

Tom joined in, backing Callista up.

"OK, let's say you're right. Why kill off ninety percent of the population? Wouldn't whoever's doing this rather have more people to fight for them? There's hardly anybody left now. It wouldn't be much of a war, would it?"

"But now the world can start afresh as the people left over are desperate and lost, and crying out for a strong leader to take control and show them the way."

Callista scoffed, raising her eyebrows. "There's pretty much nobody left alive to be leader. Those that are left are traumatised and exhausted. Nobody is in a position to govern others."

Yvonne stared at her for a moment, a frown creasing her forehead. "Callista, after the ancient war not all members of the Children of Light and the Brotherhood of Shadow died. Some carried on, survived and set up new settlements. They continued the ancient traditions, settled down in the villages and towns and had children and grandchildren. Both bloodlines survived over the years, passing down the legacy."

Callista froze. "Please don't say what I think you're going to say."

CHAPTER SEVEN

Yvonne shrugged. "Sorry, Callista. I know you don't want to hear this, but it's time. The legacy of the Children of Light passed down through the generations. Your mother was a descendant, just like you. Now the world has been purged of people again and those left alive need to follow one of two people. They will pick one of two leaders, the Children of Light leader or the Brotherhood of Shadow leader. You're the only remaining descendant of the Children of Light."

Callista stared at Yvonne, speechless. Her heart thundered in her chest. She tried to speak, but her words kept catching in the throat, which was suddenly dry and sore.

Callista looked to Tom for some comfort, but the familiar smirk was playing on his lips. His scepticism bolstered her own disbelief, and she laughed out loud.

"That's just ludicrous!"

Tom made a big show of bowing to her with an elaborate flourish of his hand. "I kneel before you, Queen Callista."

Callista sniggered but was cut short by a glare from

Yvonne. "I know this all sounds crazy, and I'm sorry you had to find out this way but—"

"OK, OK. If this is true, why didn't I know before? If my parents were some sort of leaders and I was to become one, why didn't they tell me?"

"The early descendants, the ones who emerged from the war, decided to hide who they really were. The world would expect them to lead the planet back into war. So, the survivors blended in with common people, hid their secrets and knowledge and tried to stay out of the eyes of the Brotherhood."

"Right, and my parents are descended from these survivors? That's what you're saying?"

"Not both of your parents, just your mother. The leader of the Children of Light was always female, *always*. The destiny passes down the matriarchal line. It was your grandmother then your mother and now, you."

Tom chuckled and ran his hands over his face as if he couldn't believe what Yvonne was saying. "Now I've heard it all. I knew Callista was a bit full of herself but royalty?!"

Both Callista and Yvonne cast him a glare, and he silenced his laughter by biting his lip.

"So, are there other descendants still alive today?" Callista's eyes widened, and her mouth fell open as she stared at Yvonne. "You? Are you an ancestor too?"

Yvonne laughed. "No, I'm not a descendant. I'm just a custodian of the knowledge of the ancient peoples. My job was to teach you to become the leader you would one day need to be and to teach you all you would need to know."

Callista frowned. "So, if you're not a descendant and only I am, then who exactly am I supposed to lead in this stupid war?"

The sly smile crept across Yvonne's face again. "I thought you'd never ask. Come with me." Marching off across the ruined ground, Yvonne had a bounce in her step that Callista had never seen before. The nanny, who had always been so calm and peaceful, appeared to have bolstered her spirits in a way that unnerved Callista. It was as if Yvonne had been eagerly awaiting such a cataclysmic event. But Callista and Tom dutifully followed behind her as they weaved through the broken columns and ancient stones. What else could they do? If Callista wanted answers, she would have to get them where she could.

Yvonne passed around the back of one of the more preserved buildings, a semi-circular structure that looked like an amphitheatre. At the rear of the impressive structure was a set of stone steps that led down to a system of underground tunnels and catacombs. At the bottom of the steps, Callista looked both ways, but the path to the left twisted and turned into darkness, and the path to the right was a dead end. To Callista's surprise, Yvonne walked straight up to the wall blocking their way and pushed on a stone with a strange carving on it. The wall rumbled. Then, with an almighty push, Yvonne managed to heave the heavy door open just wide enough for herself, Tom and Callista to slide through.

Apprehension prickled within Callista, but she followed with a warning knot of anxiety inside her stomach. Whatever she had been expecting on the other side of the door, it hadn't been this. There was a vast underground chamber lit by flaming torches. Most surprising of all was the group of people sat all around the room, lounging on comfortable sofas and reading books with old dusty covers. Two young girls sat together by the fire, one braiding the other's hair, chatting away happily. An old woman was carving something out of a wooden branch in the corner, and a young man appeared to be preparing food in a makeshift kitchen area at the back.

Callista couldn't believe her eyes. These people had a whole civilisation under here. This wasn't a hastily constructed base like the survivor camp. These people had been preparing for this. They had known it was coming. And what was more, they had known Callista was coming too because no sooner had the first pair of eyes settled upon her than the shouts and cries of wonder had begun. People rushed over to her, wanting to take her hand, staring at her in amazement and singing her praises. One woman even sobbed openly as large wet tears cascaded down her aged cheeks.

Bewildered by the reaction, Callista looked to Yvonne questioningly. "What is all this?"

Yvonne smiled. "These are your followers, Callista. Your people."

"My...?" Callista stammered. "I have people?"

"Oh yes. These people have been waiting a very long time for you."

The old lady who had stroked Callista's cheek was back in front of her, and Callista had to edge away from her grasping, adoring hands once more.

"Will you lead us now? Are you here to guide us?"

A young man appeared beside her. "The True Nienna is here! Finally, our saviour has arrived!"

Before Callista could utter a confused response, she was bombarded by exclamations of joy.

"The True Nienna! She's here. She's really here!"

"It's time. It's our time at last!"

"Let the ancient knowledge of the Niennas be discovered once more!"

Speechless and with a head reeling from the bizarre turn of events, Callista found herself without words. Yvonne stepped in to fill the silence.

"Callista Nienna is weary and traumatised by the trials of the last few days. Please, give her some space and time to absorb everything she needs to know." Yvonne put a gentle hand on Callista's arm and tried to lead her away from the throngs of curious and excited people. "Come, we'll explain later. Get some rest now."

Callista pushed her hand away, gently but firmly. "No. I want to know what all this is about. Why are these people speaking to me like this? Who do they think I am?"

"They don't think anything, Callista. They *know* you are the last surviving Nienna."

The vague answer did nothing to quell Callista's raging confusion and curiosity. Tom voiced the same concerns she had. "And this is about the Light Children or whatever?"

A frown crossed Yvonne's face. "These people are the followers of the Children of Light, the last followers of the ancient cult of the Light. They have been awaiting their leader for a long time. They believe it is up to the true Nienna descendant to embrace the history of their people and unlock the secrets of the temple."

This was all starting to get to Callista, whose patience for vague and mysterious ponderings was thinning. "I still don't know what the hell you're talking about! None of this makes any sense!"

"OK, OK," Yvonne said, holding up her hands in a placatory gesture. "Let me show you the temple, and maybe things will become clearer."

Callista looked at Tom who shrugged his shoulders. If she had been hoping for a quiet and personal introduction to her destiny, she was to be disappointed as the crowd of adoring people followed behind them. Yvonne led them back up some stone steps and out to the front of a large stone building with gothic, arched porticos and incredible carved pillars.

Despite the intricate designs carved into the marble, the building was clearly ancient, falling apart in places and eroded by centuries of weather. The front door itself was an immense slab of stone, carved with primitive etchings of people, animals and creatures the likes of which Callista had never seen.

There was no handle. Callista frowned, wondering how they were to enter the temple. She took a step closer and examined the door, running her fingers over the fascinating carvings. Her hand passed over a huge circle in the centre where a deep indent had been lovingly carved out of the stone. It looked like a tiny font, a stone bowl in the centre of the recess with a small hole in the bottom which disappeared into the darkness within the temple.

Yvonne stepped up beside Callista, her eyes shining with pride as she looked over the stone door. "This temple was built by the original Children of Light hundreds of years ago. It is said that inside lie the secrets to the Children of Light's power, wealth and, most astonishingly of all, their eternal youth."

Callista's eyes widened, but she couldn't tear her gaze from the stone bowl in the centre of the ornate door. "It is said? Haven't you been inside?"

"Sadly not. Nobody has for many, many years."

Tom cast his eyes over the stone door. "How do you get in?"

"That's the problem. We can't. We've never been able to open the door because," Yvonne hesitated and took a deep breath, "it's blood locked."

"Blood locked? What does that mean?" Callista asked.

"It means that it can only be opened with a drop of blood from the True Nienna, the one destined to succeed the original Nienna ruler. Your mother, Karla Nienna, tried to open the door and failed. Your grandmother was also unsuccessful. Now the Children of Light remnant camp has been awaiting the arrival of a Nienna who can open the door."

"Whoa," Tom said, holding his hands up to Yvonne. "You want Callista's blood? How much of it? How would you get her blood? If you're going to suggest hurting her, you'll have to get through me first."

Yvonne smiled with a hint of pity. "Oh, Tom. You don't need to worry. A single drop is all that would be needed. It wouldn't be any more than a simple prick of the finger."

Tom seemed placated by her reassurances, but Callista raised her eyebrows. Again it felt as if Yvonne had slipped into some surreal fantasy world. "What makes you think it takes Nienna blood to open the door? I mean, if Mum and Grandma's blood failed, doesn't that tell you the legends are nonsense?"

Yvonne's laugh was mildly condescending. "It isn't just some old nonsense we've heard in rumours. We have ancient documents that tell of the war. That is where we learnt all we know about the Children of Light and the Brotherhood of Shadow. It's how we know about the blood-locked temple and the secrets that reside within."

Tom gave a small laugh. "And nobody has been inside? Nobody thought to break the door down?" There was an audible gasp of horror from the gathered throngs behind them. Callista felt her irritation spike.

Yvonne responded with a calm clarity to her voice. "No, not for hundreds of years, not since the original leader sealed it."

"So what? You're waiting for a new messiah? How ridiculous!" Callista snorted with laughter and shook her head.

"We believe it's you."

"Why?" Callista replied, defiant.

"Because your time has corresponded with the apocalypse. According to legend, the true leader, the 'descendant of light,' will survive against all the odds and live to defeat the Brotherhood of Shadow once and for all. Don't you see, Callista? Survive against all the odds. That's exactly what you've done.

Look me in the eye and tell me there wasn't some higher power keeping you alive as you escaped Pabell?"

Memories flashed through Callista's mind of the water thundering towards her and Tom then pooling calmly at their feet. "But that's just coincidence," she muttered.

"No!" Yvonne cried, becoming more passionate as the people who had gathered around them started to sway in mesmerised worship. "It isn't coincidence at all. You found your way here, to the survivor camp, against all the odds. You're the last of the Niennas. If it isn't you, then we are all doomed."

"This is insane," Callista said, wrapping her arms across her chest and pacing backwards and forwards.

"Please, Callista. Try the door. We need to know. All of these people need to know." Yvonne waved her arm across the crowd of hopeful followers, and Callista felt her spirits drop even further. A bitter lump grew at the back of her throat, and tears welled in her eyes. Before Yvonne or the crazed worshippers could say anything more, Callista turned and pushed through the crowd. When she had broken free of the crowd, she started to run. Pushing herself harder and faster, she made her way to the edge of the ruined town, sobs heaving in her chest. When she was clear of the intrusive questions and expectations, she slumped down onto a slab of stone and held her head in her hands, fighting back the tears. It wasn't the time to cry. She had to be strong. She had no choice. Yvonne and the crowd had made sure of that. Callista wasn't allowed to be a normal kid anymore, and grief welled inside of her for the happy life she had once led.

Forcing back the biting tears, she clenched her jaw and tried to sort out the jumbled mess of thoughts inside her head. The responsibility that Yvonne was suggesting was overwhelming. She was a kid, a little sixteen-year-old with no sense of responsibility and no common sense. She had no idea how to work the oven at home.

She couldn't cook herself a meal if her life depended on it (*which it might do soon*, she thought with a dry and humourless laugh). So her family name was Nienna. So what? What difference did that make? The fabled True Nienna blood in her veins did nothing to make her stronger or cleverer. It couldn't turn her into the leader she knew she couldn't be. The whole idea was ludicrous.

There was a thread of guilt in her twisted thoughts. Would it really have been too hard to try the blood-locked door at least? It wouldn't have hurt her—just a small scratch—and then the impossible expectations of the crowd would be lifted from her young shoulders.

She knew the door wouldn't open for her, even if those back at the camp didn't believe it. Her mother had been a tough, independent woman, and Callista wasn't half the woman she had been. If it hadn't opened for Karla Nienna, why would it open for her daughter? All of those people's hopes and dreams rested on her useless shoulders. While they still lived in the naive belief that Callista was their saviour, they could be happy. They could believe they weren't doomed. But as soon as she failed to open the door, they would know it was the end. How could she do that to them?

A noise from behind startled her. She leapt to her feet, ready to confront a potential attacker. She was relieved to see Tom approach. She hadn't realised how much she needed him at that moment. As soon as her eyes rested upon his handsome features, she ran straight into his arms and buried her head in his chest.

Callista snuggled into his arms, relishing the warmth of his body against hers. He wrapped a strong arm around her shoulders and pulled her in closer. She trembled from head to toe as he planted a reassuring kiss on the top of her head and stroked her blonde hair.

The weight of everything that had happened over the past few days was dragging her down, and now the revelation that she was expected to lead people threatened to crush her.

"I don't think I can do this," Callista whispered in a breathy gasp.

Tom stroked her arm gently. "It's crazy. All of this is just crazy, and frankly, I think Yvonne is off her rocker. And those people gathered back there are a whole group of nutjobs. What they're saying is nonsense. There can't be such a thing as the True Nienna. But I've been thinking. It wouldn't be so hard just to check it out. Try the door. Just to prove them wrong if anything. And if it all did end up being real after all...well... would that be so bad? If anybody, *anybody*, in the world is fit to lead us, it's you, Callista."

"Why? I'm rubbish at everything. You always say so."

"Yeah, you are, you loser." He smiled again and cast his eyes up to the evening sky. "Callista, have you never considered why I rib you all the time?"

"Because you're a jerk?"

Tom laughed and dipped his head in acknowledgement. "True, true. But the real reason is that...I've always been kind of jealous of you."

It was Callista's turn to laugh. "You? Jealous of me? Now that is ludicrous."

"No, it's not. You were so strong when your parents died. I was a mess when mine passed away. You were exceptional in our classes, whereas I had to work really hard to get my black belt. It was just natural to you. Whenever there's an argument at school, you calmly diffuse the situation. I always end up punching someone. But most of all, as you said, I'm a jerk. I believe in myself and only myself. I won't take orders from anyone, and I can't imagine clinging to the word of some self-proclaimed messiah in our situation. But you? I'd follow your every word."

Callista was shocked into silence.

"The thing is, Callista, I can totally imagine you ruling these people, the country, the world if need be. You'd be amazing. After all, you've always ruled me."

Callista remembered all the times she had bossed him around in classes, all the beatings she'd given him for holding his training staff incorrectly. But at the same time, she remembered how much trouble he'd given her in return every time. She remembered how headstrong and independent he always was.

"Nobody could rule you, Tom."

"I don't just mean that you rule me in classes. I mean, and I know this sounds cheesy, but I mean that you ruled *me*. Everything I do is for your approval. I probably would have given up on our classes years ago if it weren't for you challenging and encouraging me. At school, I would have been expelled if you hadn't calmed me down when I lost control. Everything I do, *everything*, is for you, and it has been since the day I met you."

Callista's stomach performed leaps.

He was on a roll, his heart spilling everything he had been too afraid to say before. "When you try that door, and it all turns out to be nonsense, we can choose what we do afterwards, together. And if it turns out that you are some kind of Messiah, then I'll follow you, whatever you choose to do. If you want to accept this destiny that Yvonne says you have, then I'll stay by your side and fight with you. But if you want to run away, ignore this stupid war and live out the rest of our days in a hut somewhere, I'll do that too."

Callista placed one hand on the back of Tom's head and pulled him towards her. It was a deep lingering kiss that comforted every one of the fears and insecurities she was feeling.

She wanted to take up his latter suggestion, probably more than she had ever wanted anything in her life. Spending the rest of her life just with Tom, cuddling up to his warm body, gazing into his eyes and ignoring the decrepit state of the wider world sounded amazing. But she couldn't leave Yvonne and everybody else to suffer what could potentially be a massacre because of her selfish desire to be with a cute boy. That's if she even was this True Nienna the legends spoke of.

There was only one way for her to find out. She had to try the door.

CHAPTER EIGHT

Yvonne stood slowly, gently brushing ash from the fire off her trousers as Callista approached. The smile on her face suggested she already knew what Callista was about to say.

"OK then. Let's do this," Callista said.

Yvonne glanced over her shoulder at Tom then leant in towards her. "He's a good choice, by the way. Handsome, strong, clearly adores you."

Callista's cheeks burned red with embarrassment, but she didn't try to deter Yvonne. She was too observant not to have noticed their undeniable attraction to one another.

Yvonne continued, "And it's good that he is supporting you in this. You'll need to keep loved ones by you when the war starts."

Callista rolled her eyes, irritated by the constant references to her supposed destiny. But she couldn't deny that, as she made her way through the adoring crowds and stepped up to the carved door, her heart was pounding in her chest. Tom and Yvonne stood on either side of her, a few paces back, as an expectant silence fell across the crowd. Yvonne passed Callista a short-bladed knife. She grasped it tightly in her hand, unsure how best to make the cut. Should she rip the blade across her palm quickly or take her time to avoid damaging herself too badly? Her hesitation was making the atmosphere among the crowd even tenser, and she felt the pressure of every pair of eyes upon her back.

Nervously twisting the handle of the knife round and round in her hand, she pressed the blade to her palm but couldn't bring herself to pierce the skin. She was afraid, not of the pain but of the responsibility that could come with the consequences. When she was sure she could never manage it, and the people would eventually get tired of waiting and abandon her, she felt a warm hand upon hers as Tom's fingers closed over her own, wrapping around the handle. He gave her a nod, and together they dragged the knife slowly across her palm.

Callista inhaled at the sharp pain, and a river of deep crimson blood welled in her palm. She placed her hand in the recess and allowed the drops to trickle into the stone bowl, disappearing into the hole in the middle.

Nothing happened. Callista was uncomfortably aware of the universally held breath behind her. She heaved a sigh of relief. Yvonne and the rest of the Children of Light were wrong. It wasn't her, and she was free to live out her life with Tom.

But no sooner had she accepted her new fate, than an awful grinding screech echoed around the room. Ancient stones rubbed against each other and the door, which had remained immobile for centuries, creaked and rumbled to life. It slid to the side, leaving a narrow gap, only just wide enough to fit through. But it had opened nonetheless.

There was a gasp of wonder behind her as Callista turned to face the people, her people. A hundred pairs of awed eyes rested upon her, some welling with tears of joy and relief. Some dropped to the ground at her feet, muttering praises of "Leader" and "True Nienna." Callista could feel the shock on her face, her mouth hanging slightly open, but when she looked at Yvonne, there was no hint of surprise on her features. Callista got the impression that Yvonne had known all along that the door would open. Tom, on the other hand, was almost shell-shocked.

A middle-aged woman emerged from the crowd and gently, almost reverently, wrapped Callista's wound in a bandage, taking care not to hurt her. When she was finished, Callista thanked her, and the woman's cheeks blushed pink.

Taking a deep breath to steady her nerves, Callista turned back to the door and stepped through the opening and into the building beyond. Tom and Yvonne followed meekly behind.

Callista's breath caught in her throat. The hall was an immense cylinder with a large circular marble floor of red and white and huge walls stretching up into the sky. The walls were lined with curtains, so old they could have crumbled under the touch, made of a dust-covered scarlet material that cascaded down like a waterfall.

Callista followed the ancient curtains up to the ceiling where there was a stunning stained-glass window sheltering them, coated in dust. Each panel of glass was grey and faded, but Callista could see that at one time it would have made an impressive sight. A huge crack split the glass, and spider-webbed splinters had spread across the coloured panels, shattering the effect.

Awe and wonder filled Callista as she stared at the ceiling. She got the impression she had wandered into something far bigger than she had anticipated. Something about the majesty of this room told her that the ancient civilisation Yvonne spoke of had been powerful and important.

Tom wandered over to the walls of the circular room and pulled aside one of the heavy velvet curtains. A cloud of dust mushroomed into the air, making Callista wave her hand in front of her face as she coughed.

"Look at this!" Tom's excited voice called through the dust cloud.

When it cleared, Callista saw he was holding back the scarlet curtain to show a row of bookshelves nestled behind. Ancient grey-coated tomes sat on shelves, their covers obscured by the gloom of the dimly lit room on the heavy covering of dust. They had probably been richly coloured once, bound in vividly dyed leather with elaborate stitching, but now they were one and the same, their vibrancy lost to the ages.

Yvonne spoke in a quiet voice, "It's true. This really is the lost library of Alexiria. The legends were real. These books should chronicle everything I have told you. The tales say that the history, culture and society from the time before are written here. If you are to become a leader, you will need to read all of these books."

Callista's eyes nearly popped from her head. "All of them?"

"Oh yes," Yvonne said. "There is a lot to be learnt from the mistakes of history, Callista. Never forget that."

They continued to search the impressive library.

"It couldn't be," Yvonne gasped. She was standing by a plinth which rested at the back of the room.

"Couldn't be what?" Callista craned her neck to see what Yvonne was looking at.

The stone plinth itself held no tome, but carved into the ancient stonework were two innocuous words: *The Book*. Pinned above the words was a crumbling piece of paper held down by a rock paperweight. Callista carefully pried the flaking parchment from underneath the paperweight. All it said, in scratchy black writing, was "If Nienna history you wish to make, a leap of faith you have to take."

"Leap of faith. What does it...?" Callista muttered, but the rest of her words caught in her mouth as her gaze fell upon Tom's face. He had passed beyond the plinth and was staring at the floor with wide, terrified eyes.

"Callista...you need to look at this."

With a shudder of apprehension, Callista walked around the plinth and inhaled.

There, in the red and white marble floor, was a circular hole. She crept tentatively towards it and peered down into the darkness. The gaping maw was at least a metre wide, and the pitch blackness obscured the sides. No matter how much they squinted through the inky dark, they could make out nothing. There was no sign of how deep the hole was or how it had been made.

"Do you think the marble just degraded over time?" Callista asked.

"Not likely," Yvonne said. "Look at the rest of the room. It's in perfect condition. Everything has been preserved immaculately. Besides, the edges aren't jagged and irregular. There was no accident. This hole was cut into the floor deliberately."

A cold shiver ran down Callista's spine again. "Well stand back. We don't know how deep it goes. You don't want to fall in."

There was a peculiar distant look in Yvonne's eyes as they all stepped away from the hole's edge. Her eyes were locked onto the hole as if it held some magnetic power over her. When she spoke, her voice was hazy and quiet.

"Leap of faith. The Book..."

"What?" Callista waved a hand in front of Yvonne's face, and she appeared to snap out of her trance.

"Callista, I think I know what this is about."

A hand clasped Callista's. She turned to see Tom beside her. "Tell us, Yvonne."

Yvonne heaved a deep sigh. "The legends tell of an ancient text known as *The Book of Alcherys*. They say it was used to guide and support the leader of the Children of Light. There is a superstition that nobody can rule without it, True Nienna or not. It would be crucial to your reign, Callista. You need it if you wish to govern."

Callista laughed and shook her head, muttering under her breath about the ridiculousness of her governing anybody.

Tom took a different approach. "Cool," he said, clapping his hands together enthusiastically. "So, which one is it?" He ran his eyes over the bookshelves around the room.

Yvonne looked troubled. "That's the thing. It's none of these books. The Book is completely different, and if you saw it, you would know it immediately. That's what that note meant."

She picked up the crumbling note from where Callista had placed it and read the words aloud. "If Nienna history you wish to make, a leap of faith you have to take. It can only be talking about *The Book of Alcherys*. You won't be able to make Nienna history without it."

"OK." Callista failed to share the urgency in Yvonne's tone. "So, we find it then. Let's start looking."

"No!" Yvonne snapped, making Callista stop in her tracks. "A leap of faith."

Callista shrugged, nonplussed. "What the hell does that mean? Where would I even..." she started as realisation dawned on her. "No. No way."

Tom closed his eyes and ran his hands over his face. Evidently it had occurred to him too.

Yvonne placed a comforting hand on Callista's shoulder, but she brushed it away.

"There is no way I'm jumping down that hole. No way."

"You have no choice, Callista. You are the True Nienna, and you must rule. You can only do so with *The Book of Alcherys*, and I think it lies at the bottom of that hole." Her words had turned from soft and comforting to harsh, and Callista felt like a child being reprimanded.

"Are you crazy?" Callista said. "I'm not jumping into a hole in an ancient building. That's madness! I could be killed."

Tom began to pace back and forth behind them. "There's no way I'm letting her jump into a dark hole either. Not a chance."

"See?" Callista nodded to Tom. "He's with me. It's a stupid idea. Do you want me to die? And if I did survive, what if there's no way back out?"

"You're not thinking clearly. The powers at work here, the temple, the blood lock, the Book, everything, was developed to ensure your success. What would be the point in killing off the True Nienna after heralding her rise to power? The ancients wanted you to take possession of the Book and to emerge alive, guided by its wisdom. This is a test, like the blood lock. It is a way to ensure that only the brave and faithful can retrieve the Book, and according to legend, none are more brave and faithful than the True Nienna."

"Then I'm not the True Nienna after all, am I? Because there is no way I'm brave and faithful enough to jump into that hole."

Callista walked to the edge of the hole, laughing and shaking her head. She stopped before it and gazed into the darkness once more, smiling at the very idea of throwing herself down there.

"Then you'll need a little help..." Yvonne murmured. With both hands, she pushed Callista as hard as she could.

CHAPTER NINE

Callista screamed as she lurched forwards, grasping desperately at the air as she plummeted downwards, her shrieks following her. Tom cried out in horror above her.

Absolute terror consumed her, but it didn't last long. After a short fall, Callista landed on a marble floor, the breath knocked from her as she landed on her back. Then she was sliding. The floor was steeply slanted, and she could get no purchase on the smooth stone. All she could do was slip through the pitch darkness and hope she wouldn't crash into anything too painful at the bottom.

The marble slide twisted and turned and Callista flinched with each sudden corner she was thrown around. There was a faint light ahead which cut through the darkness in time to show Callista the end of the slide, seconds before she was thrown clear.

She landed in a crumpled heap on the cold ground, the wind knocked from her once again. Sitting up slowly, Callista checked herself over. She had some bruises and a few cuts, but she appeared to have sustained no major injuries. Her nerves had taken a battering though, and she trembled from the shock of the fall.

When she gathered her senses, Callista looked at her surroundings. She had fallen into a vast underground cavern, and the jagged, jutting rocks above her pointed down like accusing fingers. There was a cold chill, so she wrapped her cardigan close around her shoulders. A small underground lake lay deathly still like a sheet of black ice.

As far as she could tell, no passageways were leading to or from the cavern. The only way in appeared to be the marble slide she had just tumbled down.

Callista placed both hands on the smooth surface and tried to find something to grasp onto, in the hope of pulling herself back up it, but her fingers just glided over the cool stone. She took a few steps back then ran at the slide, hoping her shoes might offer some grip. But no sooner had her soles hit the stone than they slipped out from underneath her. She crashed onto her front and cried out in frustration.

Callista got to her feet, brushed herself down and tried to think of a way out. She leaned as far into the slide opening as she could and cupped both hands to her mouth.

"Tom!" she shouted as loudly as she could. Her voice echoed around the cavern. She waited a moment for a reply, but none came.

The only thing she could do was to search for the stupid book she was supposed to find. On the edge of the lake was a collection of small rounded stones, like a tiny grey beach to go with the foreboding black lake. Callista's feet crunched with each step as she followed the vague light that seemed to come from nowhere. She searched for a gap in the rock above, a glimpse of the sky maybe, where the light could be seeping in. But she found nothing. The origin of the light was just another weird mystery to add to the collection of nonsensical things that had happened to her recently.

She walked halfway around the lake and came upon a circular table cut neatly from stone. Upon it were ancient-looking wooden chunks of different shapes and sizes. Each was inscribed with strange markings, none of which meant anything to Callista. She picked up a few of the pieces and saw that they fit neatly together.

It was a jigsaw.

Excited by the prospect of a puzzle to solve, Callista set to work rearranging the pieces. Chess, jigsaws, or any kind of puzzle had always held her fascination. She had spent hours in front of her puzzles as a child. This one, however, was brutally difficult. No matter how she tried to fit the pieces together, there were always some left out or she came unravelled when another piece would no longer fit. She had no idea what the finished picture was supposed to be. Where was the picture on the box to help her out?

Her temper began to fray. She slammed the pieces down, getting cross when they didn't fit together. It was only the delicate, ancient nature of the wooden fragments that prevented her from flinging them across the cave in anger.

Without a watch to tell the time, she had no idea how long she had spent trying to fit the jigsaw together. It felt like hours. Eventually, the anger subsided, and the chill of the cave made Callista shudder.

What could she do? This stupid puzzle was too hard, and she had no idea if she was close to completing it or not. Were all of the pieces even there? There was nothing else in the cave. It was just a cold, barren no-man's-land. The only glimmer of hope came from the infuriating jigsaw.

"Right. It's time to pull myself together." She muttered aloud hoping to bolster her failing determination.

She approached the puzzle again. She tried turning the pieces in different orientations, sliding different segments together in the hope of seeing something that had eluded her before. Eventually, the pieces came together to make a circle. Intersecting lines and circles crossed the sections seemingly at random. The last piece slotted in. Nothing happened.

Callista released her breath with a heavy sigh. She slumped down to the cold, stony ground and felt a slight thump on her chest. The necklace tucked under her clothes had bumped into her skin as she crumpled. She reached into her top and pulled on the delicate golden chain. Shining gold, even in the dim cave, the necklace seemed to radiate its own light. The diamonds shimmered and brought life to the cave once more.

Callista stared at it. A golden circle with a cross in the centre embedded with diamonds. A circle with intersecting lines. She knew what the jigsaw was supposed to show.

With a rush of adrenaline, Callista jumped to her feet and began rearranging the puzzle pieces to match the design on her necklace. It didn't take long, and within minutes she was staring at a large wooden version of the jewellery she had been wearing practically her entire life. The circle had been right all along, but the pieces within it had been in the wrong places. Now the design made sense. Four crosses pointing inwards to meet in the centre where a symbol of infinity rested. Callista didn't understand what it meant, but she felt moved just by looking at it. Energy and passion flowed from the completed jigsaw, igniting something deep within Callista's heart. Something she had never even known was there.

But still, nothing happened. There was still no doorway from which to make her escape. Completing the puzzle had done nothing. Except in the very centre of the puzzle was a recess, as if a circular chunk had been cut out of the wood. Callista gasped as she realised it was the exact size and shape of the necklace itself. She placed the necklace into the recess. It fit perfectly and no sooner had the gold rested within its casing than a powerful beam of light shot up to the ceiling of the cave.

Callista shielded her eyes. When she could stand the blinding light, she peered through narrowed eyes and what she saw took her breath away.

Standing before her, shrouded in white light was Tom. But it wasn't Tom as she knew him, young and cheeky, handsome in a boyish way. This was an older version of her friend. But older wasn't the right word because he didn't seem to have aged as such. His skin was still firm and youthful, his eyes bright and shining as they were now. He looked the same age, but somehow his demeanour suggested wisdom and experience. He stood tall and proud, his shoulders back, chin raised. He was no longer dressed in his usual dark jeans and casual shirt. Instead, he was clothed in a tunic with armoured shoulder panels and iron wrist braces. He looked like a medieval knight. Embroidered in silver on the front of his tunic was the symbol from the necklace and the jigsaw.

Once the initial surprise faded, Callista threw herself towards him, desperate to feel his arms around her, but her hands grasped at thin air as she fell through him. Tumbling forwards, she just managed to stop from falling flat on her face. She whirled around, confused and bewildered.

"Tom?" she whispered. His image turned to face her. A warm smile graced his lips, and his face blurred ever so slightly. He was just a vision, a mere spectre, dust dancing in the light.

"Callista." His voice was eerily familiar. He might have been standing in the room with her right now.

"Is it really you?"

"Not the now, but the future me."

"I don't understand."

"You don't need to. For now, you need to get out of this cave alive."

Callista glanced at the cave around her. "How? There is no way out."

"Sometimes the truth hides in plain sight."

She stared at him for a moment. "What does that mean?"

The spectre of Tom raised a hand. Streams of light trailed behind it as it rose. He pointed to Callista's immediate right, but when she turned to look, nothing was there.

"What?"

"It is your way out. Up."

"But I came here to fetch the *Book of Alcherys*. I can't leave without it."

"You must make the journey to the top, and there you will find the book you seek."

Callista's eyes followed his hand as it rose again and pointed to the ceiling of the cave. There, hidden in a dark recess, was an opening. It was an exit. The only exit.

"How am I supposed to get up there? Is there a path?"

"You climb."

Callista laughed, but one look at the spectre told her this was no joke.

"You can't be serious," she said. "I can't climb a sheer wall with no ropes or harnesses. If I fall, I'll die."

"Therein lies the trial."

Staring at the wall before her, she ran her hands over the surface and was surprised to feel divots and small ledges on the rock. It wasn't as smooth as she has first assumed, but to climb it would be a death sentence.

"Trial or not, I can't do it. There must be another way."

"There is none, and time is ticking by, Callista Nienna. The trial must be completed."

Callista muttered under her breath, "I don't know why I'm

listening to you. You're not even real." But there seemed to be no other choice. It was a choice between risking the climb and dying in the cave. Starvation or hypothermia, which would come first? She didn't want to think about it.

Callista reached out and laid a hand on the cave wall. She gasped and drew back. The stone was bitterly cold and her cut hand stung like crazy, even underneath the bandage. It wouldn't be a pleasant climb. But there was no other option. Steeling her nerves, Callista reached up and found two handholds. She checked they were secure and would hold her weight and then began to climb.

Each move she made was torturous, and she was plagued by the terrible fear that she might fall onto the jagged stones below. It didn't take long for her arms to feel the strain and her fingers to become numb.

"Stay strong, Callista. You can make it." The Tom-who-was-not-really-Tom called out gentle, soothing reassurances to her. He didn't look like the boy she loved, but his voice was the same comforting sound she had longed to hear every day. Even though she knew it wasn't real, it still gave her the strength she needed to carry on.

She glanced down and immediately wished she hadn't. It felt like she had been climbing forever, but the ground was still woefully close. Far enough to break bones if she fell but not even a third of the way to the top yet. She looked up at the cave ceiling, which made her feel even worse. There was so far left to go. Exhaustion might kill her if she didn't get to the top before her arms gave up or her fingers became too numb to support her.

She was nearing the halfway point when the rock face changed. Her fingers curled around the narrow ledge and squelched onto something damp and slippery nestled behind it. She grimaced but managed to reposition her grip and pull herself onwards. That was when the dripping began. Trickles of freezing water ran over the rock and droplets fell onto her head, running into her eyes and obscuring her vision. Her foot slipped. Callista screamed and clung on for dear life, frantically trying to regain a foothold. When she thought she could hold on no longer, her toes found a tiny crevice, just enough for her to rest on for a moment, gather her breath and calm her pounding heart.

"Stay calm. You're nearly there, Callista. Then you can rest," Tom's voice echoed around her.

"I can't do this!" She sounded like a child, but that was exactly what she felt like, a little girl who was way out of her depth.

"You can!" The words boomed around her. "You are Callista Nienna, and this trial was designed for you. You can do it, and you will."

She was suddenly imbued with strength and energy. Her eyes fixed on the prize ahead, and she continued the climb.

If the first half of the climb was difficult, the second was near impossible. The wall became mossier and Callista's fingers slipped more times than she dared to count. Her heart was thundering in her chest as she neared the top. A misguided glance down to the cave floor gave her vertigo and her head span. Vowing to keep her eyes straight ahead, Callista continued pulling herself up with aching, exhausted arms.

She pulled herself over the ledge at the top, dragging her legs over to safety. Panting heavily, Callista lay on her back, squinting at the bright sky above her. When she managed to catch her breath, she rolled over and took in her surroundings. A cloudless blue sky was above her, and she shielded her eyes from the sunshine which was blinding in comparison to the dark cave she had just emerged from. There was a rough surface beneath her. It may once have been a pathway, snaking through the long, unkempt grass, but now the stones were broken. Moss and weeds poked up through the cracks as nature reclaimed its land. There were tall stone walls surrounding the small garden where she found herself, and a quick look around told Callista that this must be at the rear of the Nienna temple.

Callista got to her feet, ignoring the reluctant scream of pain from her aching muscles and the cut on her hand. She was desperate to see Tom again, to make sure he was all right, but a nagging feeling in the pit of her stomach was pulling her in the opposite direction. She followed the winding pathway and came to a stone plinth right at the back of the garden, surrounded by shrubs that concealed its hiding place. If it weren't for the odd vibes she was detecting from it, she wouldn't have known it was there.

Callista pulled vines and leaves away and there, upon the plinth, lay the oldest book she had ever seen. It was bound in leather, gilded around the edges and stunningly beautiful. Callista already knew this was important. An aura of age and wisdom surrounded it. Reverently, she picked the Book up and held it tightly to her chest as she weaved back down the garden path and made her way to the rear of the temple.

The door that would lead her back to Tom and Yvonne was yet another huge slab of stone, ornately decorated and undoubtedly heavy. It wouldn't push or pull open, and Callista had a fleeting moment of terror at the thought that she had emerged from the cave alive, only to starve to death out here. But then her eyes fell on a recess on the wall to the left side of the door. It was another blood lock. She unwound the bandage from her hand. The cut from opening the first lock had only just stopped bleeding. It was sore, and dirt from the climb had worked its way under the bandage. It was with reluctance that Callista scratched at it to reopen the wound. It soon began to flow with blood again. Callista placed the blood into the recess and the door opened.

She pushed through a dusty, velvet curtain and found herself at the back of the library once more.

"Callista!"

She barely had time to look around before Tom threw himself at her, wrapping his arms around her and burying his face in her hair.

"I thought I'd lost you. I shouted and shouted after you, but there was no reply. Are you OK?" He pulled back and began checking her injuries.

"I'm fine, Tom. I'm fine, honestly. Just a few cuts and bruises, but I'm glad to be out of there alive."

Tom hugged her again and planted a firm kiss on her lips.

"How long was I down there?" Callista asked.

Yvonne emerged from behind one of the bookcases. "Around three hours." Callista caught a bitter glare that Tom threw in Yvonne's direction.

"It felt longer," Callista said with a dry smile. "Is everything all right here?"

Tom looked to the floor and began kicking around in the dust with a frown on his face. Yvonne looked at Callista intently, her blue eyes burning into Callista's.

"Tom isn't happy with me," Yvonne replied. "He doesn't understand why I pushed you into the leap of faith."

"You shouldn't have done it!" Tom shouted, his fists clenched. "You could have killed her!"

Yvonne rolled her eyes in a manner that Callista found condescending. "We've been over this for hours, Tom. The trial wasn't designed to kill the True Nienna, was it? It was there to test her, and that's all."

"You didn't know that for sure. You said you'd never been in this temple either, so how could you have known? And even if that had been the intention hundreds of years ago, what if it had crumbled and fallen apart or something? Callista could have fallen to her death!"

Yvonne glared fiercely at Tom but had no response.

Callista felt it was time to step in. "Look, both of you, I'm fine. It worked out OK, and I wasn't harmed. I completed the trial and best of all, I got this."

She held up the Book and Yvonne inhaled, all animosity forgotten.

When Yvonne spoke again, her voice was cracked and emotional. "It's the fabled Book." She sighed as if this were a moment she had been waiting for her whole life. "This is the ancient text that the Children of Light used to live their lives by. There are hundreds of stories about the Book, but nobody knows where it came from or who wrote it. Some say it was written by the gods themselves."

Callista raised her eyebrows sceptically, but Yvonne was not deterred. "Callista, this is a monumental time for us, for you. If you are to become the leader of the Children, you will need to know this inside and out."

Callista hadn't accepted that she even was this fabled leader, but she seemed to be getting swept along in the legend. "Well, what is the Book about?"

"They say it tells the mistakes of the past and prophesizes the future."

"That's impossible, surely."

"That's for you to decide. As the True Nienna, it falls to you to accept or reject the wisdom of those who came before. But I suggest you read it thoroughly before you make any assumptions."

"Should I open it?" Callista said in a voice that was so quiet it was nearly a whisper. Yvonne nodded, and Callista tentatively reached for the brass clasp. Her heart thumped in her chest so hard she was sure she could actually hear it. She unclipped the brass hook, pulled the Book open and her eyes landed upon the first handwritten page:

The Book of Alcherys

The writing was ancient and scratchy with sharp lettering as if the words had been etched onto the pages with an old feather quill.

"*The Book of Al-cherries*?" Callista said. Yvonne cast her a frown. No doubt her error in pronunciation was some kind of blasphemy.

"It's pronounced Al-keriss," Yvonne scolded.

Callista turned to the next page, her heart pounding even faster as she read on.

Future's children, mothers of history, father's estate. Tomorrow and yesterday are forever intertwined, two linking branches coiling around the tree of life and blossoming into eternity. Alcherys stands and falls and stands again. When fire burns and sulphur streaks the skies, when the oceans consume the land and the multitudes are crushed, the living stand tall and take the helm. The one true descendant, reluctant and inexperienced, will rise to destiny. Let these words light the way to glory before pandemonium reigns again.

Weird sensations were flooding over Callista. She didn't fully understand what this Book was saying, but this message seemed uncannily reminiscent of their current situation.

When fire burns...When the multitudes are crushed. That sounded just like the apocalyptic scenes Callista and Tom had fallen victim to just days before. *The descendant, reluctant and inexperienced.* Callista's head swam. She blinked furiously to clear the fog that clouded her vision and tried to keep the contents of her stomach from leaping into her mouth.

"Cal, do you think this means you?" Tom asked.

"The descendant, reluctant and inexperienced, will rise to destiny." Yvonne smiled with warm acceptance, as though all this was perfectly normal. "Rise to destiny. It means you must take the helm, Callista. You must revive the ways of your family, your people. You are the only person on the planet able to lead the surviving realm."

Callista crossed her arms defensively across her chest.

"Don't shake your head like that, Callista, as if what I say is nonsense. You know as much as I do that all of this is real. By now, the Nienna blood in your veins will have begun to stir and the heritage that has passed down to you for centuries will be calling you to fulfil your potential."

"You keep saying that, but I know nothing! Nothing is calling me! I'm sad, I'm angry and I'm confused, but there is nothing coming naturally to me. And I am definitely NOT this leader you think I am!"

But even as she said the words, something stirred in the pit of her stomach, a peculiar churning, not quite like sickness. It was more pleasant than that.

"You may not be able to see it yet. After all, you are reluctant." Yvonne paused to give Callista a meaningful look. "But you will soon see that this is your destiny. You opened the blood lock, Callista. You are the only person in history to manage that. Of course, you're the chosen one. It cannot be disputed. This destiny is yours and yours alone. Would you want somebody else to shoulder the burden of fighting the Brotherhood? Could you trust another to do it and do it well?"

Callista was ready to shrug her shoulders and tell Yvonne she couldn't care less who did it, but before she could voice her annoyance, a burning fire rumbled deep inside of her, as if a flare had been ignited in her core. Suddenly, she was inexplicably angry, ready to leap into action that very moment and fight whatever lay in her way.

"So that's what it took?" Yvonne said. "The idea of another filling your role?"

"Apparently so," Callista replied quietly. Everything in Callista's mind, all the addled thoughts, fears and anxieties of the past few days cleared in a single heartbeat. She was consumed by an intense certainty that this was right, that this was what she had to do. But she needed to get all the facts straight.

"Tell me everything, Yvonne. Tell me who the Brotherhood really are, who I am."

"The few we have gathered here are your supporters, willing to follow the Children of Light's message, but you are the True Nienna, the last remaining Child of Light. We can search for more survivors, but if you want an army to rival the Brotherhood of Shadow, you must create it yourself."

Callista couldn't contain a panicked laugh. "How am I supposed to find soldiers? Half the world was just obliterated, and those that are left are exhausted and weak."

"They are now. But by being there for them, leading them, showing them the way, you will gain their trust and their allegiance."

"But can they really become soldiers?"

"If you take care of them, feed and clothe them, build them a city of their own, they will become whatever you want them to be." Yvonne gently took both of Callista's hands in her own. "Callista, this Book is everything. It will tell you all you need to know. Let's take it back with us to your followers, and you can come to grips with everything inside its pages."

Callista frowned. "No. It's too important. If I am to return to those people and ask them to follow me, I need to go back with something concrete. I can't expect them just to believe me.

Hell, I didn't even believe it myself until I felt it. I need to know everything there is to know. I'll stay here and read the Book from cover to cover."

Yvonne gave a calm and respectful nod, accompanied by a slight bow. "Tom and I shall bring you anything you need. Take your time, and learn it all."

CHAPTER TEN

Dusting the front cover almost lovingly, Callista took *The Book of Alcherys* in her hands and looked at it with such reverence that it could have been a god. She settled in a large, dust-coated chair in the corner and opened the Book to the very beginning. On the second page, the symbols started. Some were faded and difficult to see, but others were clear as day, as if time had never touched their pages.

All the symbols and signs were black, scratchy and beautiful. They made no sense to Callista, yet she couldn't take her eyes from them. Shields, swords, flames and feathers all wound around the edges of the pages. At the top of every leaf was one particular symbol which Callista stared at, fascinated.

It was the same symbol as had been engraved on the jigsaw in the cave. The same design as the necklace she wore. Four daggers, turned inwards, their points resting in the middle of a knot of infinity. She couldn't tear her eyes away from it. She was in a trance, unblinking, unbreathing. It was the coat of arms for the Children of Light, and she knew she would be intimately linked to it forevermore.

It took Callista two days to read most of the Book from start to finish. She didn't stop except to eat, wash in a nearby spring, and when the light outside faded, put the Book down to rest. At first light she was up again and reading. She ate up every word like she was starving for the wisdom it gave. Gradually, she began to piece the puzzle together. She started to understand who she was, what the war was about and, most of all, she understood the weight of her duty. And it was a duty. It was certainly not a choice she wanted to make, but it soon became apparent to her she had little option.

The stories and prophecies within the Book were fascinating. It reminded her of reading the tales of old from her childhood. Tales of warring countries, cunning tricks used to win battles, fantastical creatures of terrible power and journeys of epic scale. Had she been reading all of this for entertainment, she would have laughed and cried along with the tales, but instead, she soaked it up with a numb inevitability. These were not mere fairy tales. They were true, every word. And a great many of them were prophecies about horrors to come.

They were written in riddles, beautiful and inspiring, but confusing. Callista barely understood a word, but the tone was unmistakable. They spoke of doom and death, hatred and vengeance. Each prophecy had a title, scratched in faded black ink at the top, and many were accompanied by the same drawings and symbols that she saw around the edges. But it was the titles themselves that scared her, for she knew they foretold things from her future, terrors she would have to overcome. The Prophecy of Blood, The Patterned Beast, The Traitorous Serpent. Not one of them sounded like something she would look forward to facing.

She took deep breaths to calm the panic. After all, despite the terrible things the prophecies spoke of, there was no reassurance they would ever come to pass, and if they did, it could be years from now when she finally had an army. She decided instead to focus upon the more pleasant things written within the Book. It spoke of the leader of the Children of Light, beautiful and strong. It also mentioned her first husband, the mighty warrior Scorpio. That part confused and intrigued her. Who was this man she would marry? She was excited, but her heart ached as she realised that if this Book spoke the truth, she wouldn't end up with Tom.

The thought churned inside of her, and she pushed it aside to read on. The Book spoke of her children, her many, many children and grandchildren. Callista's mind boggled at how she was supposed to have so many of them. She would have to be pregnant every year of her life to have them all. And if that was the case, how would she ever be fit to lead? None of it made any sense, and a small part of her wanted to laugh at the ridiculous Book and its illogical contradictions.

When Callista had had enough she put the Book back on its stand. Stretching her arms and legs, and arching her aching back, she left the library and made her way back outside to the makeshift camp Tom and Yvonne had set up.

"Callista. Is everything OK? Did you reach the end of the Book?" asked Tom. She smiled and pulled him towards her in a kiss.

"I just needed a break. I haven't quite reached the end yet, but I'm nearly there. A few more hours should do it."

He ushered her towards a log where he had been sitting, but Callista shook her head. "I've been sitting forever. My body is killing me. I need to keep moving."

He grinned, his eyes flashing mischievously. Then he was off, sprinting out of the camp, leaping over logs and fallen columns on his way through the ruins. He shouted over his shoulder, "One perimeter of the city. Last one back makes dinner!"

"Cheat!" Callista screamed as she catapulted herself after him, laughing.

She pushed herself on, faster and faster, her long blonde hair flowing behind her in the wind as she sprinted at full speed through the ruins. Tom had a head start, but she wouldn't let him win that easily. It felt like she was flying and she drank in the freedom, enjoying the familiar burn of her muscles as she pushed herself to her limits. Callista knew she would ache the next day, but at the moment nothing in the world mattered except stretching herself to speeds she had never reached. Before she knew it, she was gaining on Tom, who occasionally looked back over his shoulder, laughing and goading her.

She was desperate to overtake him, but he wheeled into the encampment first to a disapproving glare from Yvonne. Callista shot up to the finishing line where he waited with his hands on his sweaty hips.

Callista barrelled into him, knocking them both down. They landed in an awkward heap, both laughing uncontrollably. She hadn't laughed so hard in a long time. She tucked herself into a ball, knees pulled up to her chest, trying to stop the ache in her stomach from laughing so hard. Eventually, the laughter died down. She opened her eyes again, gathering her breath to see a bemused grin from Tom, who lay on his back, propped up on his elbows, watching her.

"It's been a while since you've laughed like that," he said, unable to contain his own beaming smile.

"There's so much pressure on me right now, I think I've gone a bit hysterical."

"You've always been hysterical. Do you remember when you cried because you lost a game of cards and wouldn't talk to me for days?"

"That's not my fault! You cheated, remember?" Callista's

lips curled in a smile. She shuffled closer to him on the dusty ground.

"Yeah, well, whether I cheated or not, you were still hysterical."

Callista elbowed him in the ribs, making him grunt. "So, you admit you cheated then?"

He pretended to be tough and squared up to her. "Yeah, what of it?"

Callista burst into laughter again and rested her head on Tom's chest, her own heartbeat calming as she listened to his reassuring thump. He gently stroked her head, and her scalp tingled. She hadn't realised just how tired she was. Before she knew it, she was drifting off into sleep, comforted by Tom's gentle caress.

CHAPTER ELEVEN

Her dreams were full of battles. Shining steel swords, bronze-plated shields and the thunder of horses' hooves. Callista saw herself riding into battle at break-neck speed, fierce and determined, sporting stunning golden armour, with Tom at her side on a black stallion. His armour was golden too, fitted to his strong physique, his body more muscled than it was now but just as striking and handsome. The army they rode towards were terrifying in their grey and black, fearsome warriors and beasts the like of which she had never seen.

Callista awoke with a start and was immediately comforted by a reassuring gentle hand from Tom. She jerked up, staring around wildly, looking for the creatures that had frightened her. Her heart gradually began to slow its rapid thundering when she saw nothing but the reassuring glow of the evening fire. Across the other side of their camp was Yvonne. She had glanced up when she'd awoke but hadn't looked surprised. Callista wondered if Yvonne had known she would go through this once she accepted her destiny.

Callista ran her hands over her face and stroked her hair back down, calming the wild strands that ran astray.

"Lie back down. Get some more rest," Tom said quietly, stroking her arm.

Callista shook her head. "No, I need to get to the end of this. I have to know everything. There's still so much that doesn't make sense."

Despite the protesting appeal in Tom's eyes, she dragged herself to her feet and made her way to the library, hoping to catch a few more hours of evening light before the darkness made it impossible to read. She picked up *The Book of Alcherys* again, amazed at how much she already felt connected to the pages and the tales they told, even to the people they spoke of. Her sons and daughters, her husband, Scorpio. They were beginning to feel like real people to her. And the places that the Book described were taking shape in her imagination—Alcherys, the nation of the Children of Light, and its capital Alexiria. The more she read, the more Callista became engrossed in the world of the Book.

She stopped abruptly when a page caught her eye. At the top, in the same scratchy black writing, was one simple word: *Elixir*. Below was a drawing of a beautiful crystal bottle with a rich golden liquid inside it.

Callista's eyes widened as she read the perplexing description:

This mystical brew has the power to stop the turning of the tides and the decline of the living. But one sip and the drinker shall never age, never fall victim to withering skin or greying hair. An eternity of youthfulness awaits he who drinks from the potion of life. Even on the verge of death itself, this tonic can bring a person back from impending oblivion. But beware. Once the damage is too great, and the icy hand of death clasps around the heart, not even the properties of the elixir can bring life back.

An eternity of youthfulness? Surely that couldn't be true? More than everything else she had read, that made Callista's head reel. Something like that could only be the subject of fairy tales. But, as with all the other things she had read, something deep in Callista's heart told her it wasn't just make-believe. If the rest of the Book told the truth, why should this section lie?

"It's all true." The voice behind Callista startled her. She jumped, nearly dropping the Book in shock. She wheeled around to see Yvonne.

When Callista had caught her breath, she scoffed in annoyance. "Come on, Yvonne. The rest of the stuff, yeah, but this? This is just crazy."

"Why?"

"A potion that can keep you young forever? That means you would never die."

"No, it doesn't. The tales of old say that our ancestors lived for thousands of years. The Elixir of Light, as it was known, offered eternal youth, not immortality. It prevented your cells from degenerating, but they were still vulnerable to external damage. That's what I was told."

"So you could still get hurt, like being stabbed or something?"

"Exactly. The drinker can still be killed in battle, but aside from that, they will never age. Callista, this is not just some story. I think it's true."

Callista didn't know whether to laugh because it was so ludicrous, or cry because everything she knew about the world was being turned upside down.

"Where is this elixir?"

Yvonne gave a mysterious, sideways grin. "I suspect that the secret to its creation lies right here, in the temple."

"OK, so where?"

"Well," Yvonne began theatrically, pulling another book

from one of the shelves, "while you were in the cave below us, I found this. Take a look."

Callista reached out and took the book from Yvonne. "What is it?"

"I think it's a recipe."

"For this elixir thing?"

"Yes. It's written in the same style and by the same hand."

Callista opened the book and cast her eyes over the list of ingredients on the first page. It was indeed the same writing, and the pages had the symbol of the Children of Light at the top. It looked as though Yvonne might be right.

"So, I have to follow this recipe, and make the elixir?"

Yvonne nodded, and Callista saw desperation in her eyes, a hunger for something. It unnerved her, so she turned back to the book.

"Let's gather these ingredients and then we can start." Though the writing had been scribed clearly in the scratchy black letters, it had still faded with time.

Elixir of Light.

Beneath it was a list of words: *nightshade, tulip, sage, sodium, Nienna, time fragments, ivy.*

Her forehead creasing with concentration, Callista bent down for a closer look at the intricately spiked and curled lettering. Many of these things could be foraged in the woods outside the ruins. It wouldn't take long to find most of the herbs and plants. But there were some items on the list that she didn't understand.

Her stomach performed a leap. "Nienna? It needs to include a part of...me?"

"Don't worry," Yvonne laughed. "I'm sure it just means it has to be mixed by the True Nienna. That's all."

Callista frowned, unsure, but moved on. "Time fragments?" she asked Yvonne. "What does that mean?"

Yvonne gave her another smug, knowing grin. "Didn't you wonder how a recipe could make somebody eternally youthful? In order to slow time down enough to halt the signs of ageing, the elixir must include small slivers of the dimension that controls time itself – The Time Realm."

"OK...," Callista hesitated. "And how the hell am I supposed to get that?"

For the first time since entering the temple, it was Yvonne's turn to look concerned. "That may be a problem. The legends state that the fragments of the ancient Time Realm lie all around us, but they are unrecognisable to mere mortals. To the average eye, they appear as ordinary stones. But to the True Nienna, their true glory shines through."

Callista blinked and took in Yvonne's words. "I 've to look around and hope I see them? But surely I've been this True Nienna all my life, and I've never seen any weird glowing stones."

"But now you know what you're looking for, Callista. I believe there's an old storage room somewhere beneath the temple. Again, that's what the legends say. Maybe the fragments will be there."

"That'd be a good place to start. I'll grab Tom, and we can all look."

Yvonne put a hand out to block Callista from leaving. "He's sleeping. Let's leave him and just us two look for now."

Something about her tone was strange, but Callista couldn't put her finger on it. With a mystified look at Yvonne, she reluctantly agreed.

The library was by far the largest room dominating the temple, but there were a few small cupboards and storerooms branching off from it. Callista hoped they would find the ingredients they needed in one of them, but there were only piles of dust and ancient crumbling tools and paper. At the back of one of the storerooms was a tiny passageway. Callista edged sideways through it and found herself in a bare, circular room.

Just across from where she stood, she saw the edge of what looked like a trapdoor with a small silver handle embedded in the wood.

"No way," she whispered with awe.

Squatting down beside the trapdoor, Callista used all her strength to yank on the handle. The trapdoor opened with a cloud of dust. Callista waved her hands in front of her face, coughing.

"Yvonne!" she yelled and a few moments later she appeared.

"After you," Yvonne said, indicating the stone staircase leading down into the darkness.

Callista baulked at the thought of going into such a dark and scary place again without a torch to guide her way, but she still stepped into the icy cold oblivion of the cellar.

Placing each foot tentatively on the stone steps, Callista made her way down into the cellar. She stepped aside, feeling behind her with outstretched hands and making sure her back was to the wall.

Callista heard the striking of a match, smelt a whiff of sulphur and watched as a tiny flame appeared a few metres away from her. Yvonne held the match out to a torch which hung on the wall. It ignited at once and revealed a long passageway flooded with yellow light.

The passage was cold, the stone damp from having no exposure to the sun in hundreds of years. The air was stale with age and the ground dirty underfoot. Before long, the stone passage opened into a wider, taller corridor that was considerably more beautiful than the previous one. Where the stone passage had been dirty and grey, this one had been looked after and decorated with care and attention. Marble rectangles were embedded in the floor, and Callista's footsteps echoed in the long passage. The walls were the most fascinating, though. Huge murals and tapestries hung gracefully on the walls flanking the corridor. Faded and worn, they looked old but the passing of time had done nothing to dampen their beauty. Hands of considerable skill had stitched and painted these adornments, and each one seemed to tell a story.

The same themes appeared time and time again as she walked down the corridor. She examined the stunning works of art: creatures with huge white wings, monsters with bat-like black protrusions, gallant warriors on horseback and people gathered around a woman with long blonde hair who looked a little like Callista herself. She stopped and stared at one particular image of the blonde woman, regal and stunning, but with a gash across her palm and blood dripping from it into a green bottle on the floor. It was uncannily like the deep slice Callista had made across her own hand to open the blood lock.

She continued, and the tapestries gave way to small marble statues of many people (the enigmatic woman from the tapestries had been depicted here too) and creatures of unusual proportions and features. Callista's eyes roamed over each one in turn, marvelling at the craftsmanship, until she came to a life-size wooden mannequin that stood guard outside a closed wooden door.

The mannequin, which had no features, but a smooth wooden ball for a head, was dressed in an impressive suit of armour. But this was nothing like the armour Callista had seen in the museums she visited with Yvonne or her parents as a child. Where those had been bulky and heavy metal, shining and silver, these were deep black with incredibly strong fibres so tightly woven into the fabric that it was like an armoured bodysuit. It would have fit the wearer snugly, probably tailored uniquely for his build. Callista might have assumed it was the armour of the blonde woman, but though the waist was slim, the shoulders and upper arms were broad like those of an athletic man.

Callista ran her fingers over the tough but flexible fabric and saw a faded plaque on the wall behind her. She wiped a finger across the rusty metal plate and could just make out two letters at the beginning of a word. "Ku" was all she could see.

Her attention turned now to the wooden door that stood before her and, with an encouraging nod from Yvonne, she pushed on the doorknob and it creaked open.

Callista's breath caught in her throat, and her jaw dropped. Before her, in piles at least twice her height, were millions of golden coins. Callista stepped forwards in wonder, her eyes roaming over the coins, which shone in the firelight, glinting appealingly.

"Where did all this money come from?" Callista asked, her voice a breathy whisper.

"Didn't I mention? Your ancestors were rich. Unimaginably rich. They left this here for their descendants who would need funding to fight the Brotherhood again. Of course, they didn't know that when the modern age took over the currency would change. So, all this money has stayed here, unusable."

Callista plucked a single coin from the pile. It was heavy, much heavier than the standard coins she was used to. Engraved in the deep, yellow metal (which she was sure was solid gold) was the same symbol she had seen inscribed around the edges of *The Book of Alcherys*. It beckoned to her, pulling her in.

"Yvonne, if this Children of Light thing is real, if I really am to lead an army, I want this to be our crest." She held the coin out to Yvonne, who nodded and smiled, seemingly pleased with Callista's choice.

Callista turned the coin over and over in her hand. "These

coins are beautiful, Yvonne, but shall we just leave them here? After all, like you said, they're worthless to us.

Yvonne chuckled. "Callista, it's your world now. We are going to rebuild civilisation from scratch, exactly as you want it. Money can be whatever currency you choose."

Callista's eyes widened as the full implication of Yvonne's statement hit her. She was in charge. She would make all the decisions from now on, and she was stinking rich! She just hoped that her people, those huddled outside the temple and the survivors back at the camp, would accept her decisions and the new money she brought to them. She had a hundred questions floating around in her mind that she was desperate to ask, about her family, her legacy, the previous civilisation that had used these golden coins. But now was not the time.

Callista walked around the huge piles of coins, her mouth hanging open at the wondrous sight. Then, behind the piles, glistening through the gloom, barely lit by the torch's flame, she saw another wooden door, barely visible behind the huge stacks of golden coins. They made their way over to it, taking care not to knock over the carefully stacked treasures. Callista headed in first, pushing the door open and taking a step inside the new room.

This area was much smaller, and the claustrophobic quarters reminded Callista of a storage cupboard. There were no windows and only a few shelves lining one wall, aside from the tapestry on the opposite side. It was another tapestry of the young blonde woman. Her hand, facing towards the artist, showed the same deep gash as the tapestries on her way in.

Blue dots danced around the woman like tiny fairies or shimmering sapphire snow.

"Time fragments," Yvonne said.

"They're blue?"

"Apparently so. I've never seen them myself, but there are many accounts of their beauty."

The beautiful painting transfixed Callista, but she was also all too aware that the room held none of these stones.

"But Yvonne...there aren't any of them here. I thought this was where they would be."

"No, it doesn't look like they're here, does it?" Yvonne's expression darkened. "Well, we'll have to go and look for them, won't we? Come on, Callista. Let's go outside and search the ruins."

Callista wasn't ready to give up on the cellar just yet. She pulled a face and ignored Yvonne's comments. She returned to the recipe again, which she'd brought along for any extra insight it might have to offer.

The ingredients list was basic and offered no extra help at all, whereas the detailed instructions on the following pages were incredibly complicated. It made Callista's head pound just looking at the careful calculations and exact timings that were needed to brew this damn thing. Scanning over the first page of instructions, Callista caught a hint of how to find the time fragments.

Once the second trial has been initiated and faith leapt once more, the fragments will reveal themselves to the True Nienna, but only when treachery has passed.

Second trial, faith leapt. There was to be another trial for her to complete in order to gather the fragments.

She would have to jump into the cave again.

* * *

It took Callista an hour of arguing with Tom before he was ready to let her attempt the second trial. He had been bewildered that she would even consider it. He had begged and pleaded for her to at least rest for a few days, a few hours even. But Callista couldn't ignore the incessant pull at her heart. This needed to be done, and it needed to be done now. There wasn't any time for procrastination. She couldn't risk losing her nerve. Once Tom's shock had passed, it was replaced by anger, mostly at Yvonne.

"This is your fault! Did you talk her into this?" he yelled.

Yvonne held her hands up in surrender. "This has nothing to do with me. I didn't even know what she'd read. She just got up and left, and then I came out here, and she's talking about doing a second trial."

"Well, she's not doing it," he said, crossing his arms over his chest.

"Tom," Callista said firmly but gently. "It's touching that you care for me, really it is. But this is my decision, and mine alone. You can't do anything to stop me. Besides, I don't need you to protect me. I can look after myself." She grinned at him, hoping to slip back into their old joke, but Tom wasn't entertaining any of her playfulness. He glared at her and turned his back.

"That's OK. I understand. I'll be back soon. I promise." Callista placed both hands gently on his shoulders and whispered into his ear. "Wait here for me, and I'll be back before you know it."

His resolve gave in. He turned and kissed her, and with a final frown, let her go.

CHAPTER TWELVE

The leap of faith wasn't anywhere near as intimidating the second time around. And now Callista knew exactly where the hole led, it was less of a leap of faith than a leap of inconvenience. Jumping into the cave again was the last thing she wanted to do right now, when she was exhausted, and her mind was filled to bursting point with old legends and prophecies. Taking a deep breath, Callista sat down on the edge of the hole and eased herself in feet first. She slid down the slope once more and soon felt her feet crunching onto the stone beach below.

She gasped. The beach looked completely different from before. Gone were the scattered grey stones and in their place was an array of multi-coloured gems. The cave was lighter now too, as the colourful stones reflected what little light there was.

It was stunningly beautiful.

Callista looked up to the ceiling of the cave, where coloured beams of reflected light danced across the dark stone. There was something special happening here, something magical, and she was a part of it. The thought thrilled her.

After a wander around the cave, admiring the stunning light display, Callista set to work on her task. She had to locate these time fragments, which were apparently shards of coloured stone. How was she supposed to identify one coloured stone amongst hundreds of thousands? Callista scanned the beach hoping something would stand out, but every stone looked beautiful and mystical to her.

She cast her mind back to the portrait on the wall of the temple. The blonde-haired leader of the Children of Light had been surrounded by floating blue lights, like fireflies. Callista dropped to her knees on the beach and ran her hands through the stones, scooping up handfuls of the colourful pebbles and shards. They glittered through her fingers like multi-coloured rain as she filtered out the blue ones.

There were three blue gems in her first handful, all a slightly different shade and texture. None of them looked remarkable or stood out. She frowned, unsure what to do next. Was she expected to go through every blue stone on the beach? That would take her years. And even then she didn't really know what she was looking for. How would she recognise a time fragment if she found one?

She slumped back on the stones and tried to get her head straight. This was called a trial for a reason. It wasn't supposed to be easy, just as the first one wasn't. It was designed to test her, to check she was worthy of finding the ingredients and brewing the elixir. Whoever or whatever set up this elaborate process had a definite idea of who they wanted to pass the tests.

The jigsaw had required patience, the slimy wall strength and courage. But what was this trial testing? Her eyesight? No, that couldn't be right. Was she expected to show strength by carrying armfuls of stones around?

Or maybe it wasn't testing a quality of hers at all. Perhaps it was testing her birthright, just as the blood lock had done. And the jigsaw wouldn't have opened at all if she hadn't placed the necklace in it. A necklace only a Nienna would have possessed. This might be another way of checking an intruder hadn't broken in, as only *she* could find these fragments.

No sooner had the thought passed through her mind than she felt the beach beneath her vibrate. Callista placed her hands on the stones, and the shaking intensified. But it didn't feel like an earthquake. It was the stones themselves moving. Reds, golds and greens fell away, moving aside as a single stone rose through the pile and leapt into Callista's hand.

It pulsed in her hands, emitting shining blue light. This stone wasn't reflecting the rays of the sun. It produced its own ethereal glow. It continued to vibrate as Callista stared at it, amazed. There was no doubt about it. This was a time fragment. But one was surely not enough. Sure, she could come back for more, but what if the beach changed every time she jumped through the hole? She would have to find as many as she could now.

She walked up and down the beach, holding her hand out in front of her. When she felt a vibration, she stopped and allowed the stone to work itself free and fly to her. One by one she took the fragments back to the bottom of the leap of faith and placed them in a pile upon a large flat rock that lay there. The pile became larger as Callista's confidence grew. It was exciting, and she couldn't deny it made her feel powerful.

She held both arms out wide, closed her eyes and concentrated. Vibrations began to pulse all around her, and she used her mind to target them. All across the beach stones shifted and fell away as blue fragments rose into the air and hovered, ripe for the taking. Callista walked the beach, collecting them before placing them with the others. She was just placing three final stones when a hand reached down and snatched them from her grasp.

Callista yelped. Her eyes widened, and she stood up straight, her heart pounding in her chest. Standing before her was Yvonne with three blue time fragments clutched in her hand.

Callista was delighted to see her. "I did it, Yvonne! I did it! The fragments were calling out to me. I could feel them. They just rose into the air. I found them!"

Callista expected to see excitement or pride in Yvonne's eyes, but her nanny's expression was blank and cold. The face that had always glowed with warmth was now detached and harsh. Callista didn't understand what was happening. She took a step back and spoke again.

"Yvonne? Are you OK? What's wrong?"

There was still no response.

"What are you doing down here? Why did you follow me? I thought the trials were only for Niennas." Callista's voice shook as she spoke.

The blankness in Yvonne's eyes shifted from cold and detached to ferocious, animalistic even.

Yvonne looked down at her hand and started to play with the three fragments she was holding. She rolled them around and looked at them with fascination. When she spoke again, her voice was different, like a distant echo.

"Yes, you did it, Callista. You found the time fragments. Thank you. I never would've been able to get them if it weren't for a Nienna finding them for me. In fact, I wouldn't have even gotten into the temple at all if it weren't for that lovely Nienna blood."

Callista's heart was thundering in her chest.

Yvonne continued, "Speaking of Nienna blood, that's the last ingredient I need to brew this elixir."

Callista took another instinctive step backwards. "Why do

you need to brew it? I thought we were going to do it together. Why are you saying this?"

With a dry chuckle that made Callista shudder, Yvonne pulled a knife from her belt. "The thing is, Callista, the Children of Light have always been the privileged ones throughout history. I think it's time the Brotherhood of Shadow had some elixir too."

"You?" Callista gasped. "You're with the Brotherhood?"

Yvonne laughed. "No. I'm not part of either of your pitiful little groups. I'm something bigger. I'm above petty squabbles, but I think the war should be fairer this time around."

"If you're not a member of either army, why do you care if things are fair or not?"

Her expression darkened. "That's none of your concern, but for now, neither the Children of Light nor the Brotherhood of Shadow can be stronger than the other." She grinned again, and a gleeful sadism replaced the darkness in her eyes. "Enough talk."

Yvonne lunged at Callista with the knife, making her shriek and jump backwards, the knife narrowly missing her stomach.

"I don't understand!" Callista cried. "What are you doing? Yvonne, it's me. It's Callista. You've looked after me since I was a baby." Tears started to flow, and her voice became strangled and pained. "I was so happy when I learnt you'd survived. Why are you doing this to me?"

Yvonne jabbed the knife at Callista again as the blade sliced through her shirt and sank into her arm. She jerked away from her with a yelp of pain, blood running over her fingers. She looked at Yvonne, bewildered. All the training she had been given was worth nothing at that moment. Even the supposedly real-life fighting sessions Tom had given her on the journey went out of her head. Her mind was racing, but none of her thoughts made any sense.

"Please, Yvonne, stop this."

Yvonne laughed and stabbed at her again. Callista twisted aside to avoid the blade, but her ankle slipped on the stony beach, and she fell to the ground.

Pleading with wide, wet eyes, Callista looked up at her nanny. "Who are you? You're not Yvonne. What have you done with her?"

"The real Yvonne outlived her usefulness a long time ago. But this disguise has had its uses."

While the imposter gloated, Callista staggered to her feet. She swung for the person who wore Yvonne's appearance, but she dodged easily and countered with another brutal stab of the knife. Callista held both hands up to protect herself as the knife sliced across her palm and reopened the gash she had used to open the temple. Callista cried out in pain as the sore skin was torn open again.

Yvonne's eyes locked onto the blood running over Callista's hands. "Blood. That's all I need from you. You're no good to me dead. I need you to lead the Children of Light if my plan is to succeed."

"Plan? What plan?" Callista shrieked.

"It'll become clear with time, I'm sure. But I need your blood, Nienna."

Callista was horrified at what she was hearing. She clutched her wounded hand to her chest, but blood was still pouring from the cut on her arm as well. Large crimson droplets fell to the ground and splashed across the stones, painting them red.

Yvonne was mesmerised as the blood fell. She gazed thirstily at the scarlet splashes. Callista saw that Yvonne was distracted and took her chance. Using her good arm, she lashed out and punched Yvonne hard across the face, knocking her to the ground with a yelp of pain.

Callista ran as soon as Yvonne fell. She sprinted across the beach, praying she would keep her footing and not slip or stumble. Fate was on her side, and she made it across the beach. The time fragments were still piled up at the bottom of the leap of faith. Callista grabbed as many as she could carry, scooping them up into both arms and cramming them into her pockets. Yvonne still had the few she had swiped, but there was nothing Callista could do about that now. There was no way she was going back over to the callous monster who had stolen her nanny's identity.

She needed to find a way out. A gut-wrenching thought occurred to her. The only way out was the mossy wall she had climbed before. She could have cried and collapsed to the ground in despair but she had to carry on. She was the True Nienna, and somewhere above, her people were waiting for her return.

Running as fast as she could with arms full of stones, and trying not to drop too many of them, she sprinted to the sheer rock face.

What she saw when she got there made her cry out with relief. Where the near-impossible climb had been before was now a stone staircase. She was more grateful than mere words could ever express. She took the steps two at a time, ignoring the fragments that fell from her grasp. She had hundreds in her arms. A few less wouldn't matter. It was more important that she survived.

At the top of the stairs, Callista turned and looked for Yvonne. She had been afraid she might be right behind her, perhaps crawling up the steps one at a time, dragging her way after her. But she hadn't moved from where she had fallen. Collapsed upon the stony beach, Yvonne was running her hands over the splatters of Callista's blood on the shards of coloured stone. She unleashed an unearthly cackle that drifted across the beach.

Callista shuddered. Her nanny was gone. She was just about to leave the cave, hopefully forever, when Yvonne's eyes locked onto her.

With a deadly sneer, she distorted into a billowing cloud of darkness. Her entire body was engulfed in the twisting smoke, and she disappeared into thin air. The only sign she had been there was a smeared handprint in Callista's blood.

Callista turned and ran.

CHAPTER THIRTEEN

Callista wound her way back through the temple, passing through the library and out of the front door in a state of shock.

Pacing backwards and forwards outside was Tom. As soon as he saw her, he ran over and wrapped his arms around her.

"My God, Callista. I thought you were dead. Are you OK? Yvonne..."

"I know," she said weakly. There was a deep gash running down the side of Tom's face. She reached out a loving hand, and he clasped her fingers in his.

"Where is she? She went in after you. I tried to stop her, but she just battered me aside."

Callista's knees gave way as she collapsed to the ground, spilling the time fragments.

"Are you OK?" Tom repeated. "You're hurt." His eyes widened as they ran over the gashes on her arms. "We need to get you bandaged up."

Callista waved away his attentions. "No. Not right now. There are more important things to worry about."

"But—"

"Please, leave it. It looks worse than it is."

He tried to argue again, but she cut him off with a fierce glare.

"Look, Tom. I did it. I found the time fragments."

As if seeing the blue stones for the first time, Tom stared at them. He picked one up and turned it over in his hand, examining it.

"Is this really a time fragment? It isn't that special."

"Trust me." She didn't have it in her to give any more of an explanation.

"What about Yvonne?" Tom asked, glancing back at the temple entrance.

"She found me down there. It was Yvonne, except it wasn't. I don't think it's been her all along." The words hurt to say.

"What do you mean?"

"She just looked like Yvonne, but it wasn't really her. It was an imposter. Whatever it was, it used Yvonne's face as a disguise. Beneath, it was...a monster."

Callista couldn't look at Tom. She didn't want to see any scepticism. She didn't want him to look at her like she was mad. How could he possibly believe her? Nobody in their right mind would.

"I thought there was something wrong with her. It was the way she pushed you at the leap of faith. It just wasn't like her. Monster or not, she wasn't right."

Tears welled up in Callista's eyes, and she met Tom's gaze. There was no ridicule, no mockery.

"You don't think I'm crazy?"

He gave a crooked, charming smile. "I'm not sure about the imposter stuff, but it wouldn't be the craziest thing that's happened in the past few days, would it? There's definitely something wrong with Yvonne. I'll give you that. Let's see when she comes out."

"I don't think she's coming out. We fought down there. I only just managed to get out."

"Did she try to hurt you?"

"Yes." The word caught in Callista's throat, and she swallowed her pain. "But she didn't want to kill me. She just needed my blood, as the final ingredient for the elixir."

The shock and anger Tom felt was evident in his bewildered expression. "Your blood?"

"Yes."

Everything that had happened in the last few days seemed to crush down upon Callista's shoulders at once. She wrapped her arms around Tom's shoulders and wept. They stayed that way for a long time until she had cried every last tear. Tom stroked her hair and held her tightly as she sobbed for Yvonne, for Pabell and for the life she had known.

When the wracking sobs ended, Callista finally sat up, wiping her eyes, and faced Tom with renewed strength.

"It's just you now, Tom. You're all I have left."

"And I'll be here for as long as you need. Always, if you want that."

Callista smiled, thankful that he was with her at that moment.

"Look, Tom. Yvonne said she was taking the time fragments and my blood to the Brotherhood. She said it was time for them to rule for once."

"No! If the Brotherhood gets the elixir, we're doomed."

"No, not doomed. We just need to make sure we make it for our people as well. That way, at least we'll have a chance."

Tom smiled. "That's my girl. Let's go brew ourselves an elixir."

* * *

It took a few hours to gather the set of ingredients they needed, and Callista was extremely thankful for the times Yvonne had taken her out in the woods as she was growing up, getting her to name plants and herbs. She was struck by sadness at the thought of her nanny, even more so by the horrific creature who had worn her appearance. It was a terrible fate for anybody to suffer, but for it to be the one she loved most was too painful for Callista. She tried to concentrate on the positives, to remember Yvonne as the loving mother-figure she had always been, but the memories were tainted now.

Callista's memories of her parents didn't seem the same now she knew who she really was. She was constantly reminded of the fact that all the innocent, fun things she did as a kid were intended to train her for this moment in her life. The ordinary life she thought she had led hadn't been so ordinary after all.

Tom bent down to pick up a spiky branch from a shrub that grew close to the ground. Upon it were bright purple berries that looked ripe and delicious. Callista knew better than to eat wild fruit without knowing what it was, but she couldn't deny it looked appealing in her current tired and hungry state.

"That's the last of it," Tom said with a smile.

Callista wiped the gathering sweat from her forehead. "OK. Let's head back and see if we can mix this up."

"Will it really stop you from ageing?" Tom asked.

Callista shrugged her shoulders. "None of this seems real to me. I keep expecting to wake up from this crazy dream at any moment and find myself back in my comfortable old life. There have been so many insane things happening these past few days, maybe this is just the latest surprise."

They carried the new ingredients, along with the time fragments, back to the temple entrance and set it all out in front of them. The recipe lay beside them, and they studied it carefully.

It was difficult to read and even harder to understand. After fifteen minutes of trying to decipher the first line, Callista ran her hands over her face, frustrated.

"How the hell am I supposed to brew this damn thing if I can't even read the instructions? What if I do it wrong? It could kill me!"

"Callista, tell me again how you found the time fragments."

She frowned, recognising where he was going with this. "I just sort of...sensed them, and they came to me. They were vibrating."

"OK, so can you do the same thing again here?"

"I didn't do it on purpose before. It just... happened."

"It may be our only option."

Callista had to admit that he had a point. What other choice did they have? She closed her eyes and held her hand out over the ingredients. Nothing happened. She concentrated as intensely as she could. Still nothing.

"This is ridiculous!" she snapped. "I can't feel a thing!"

"OK, fine. Forget that. We'll have to try to read it." Tom picked up the recipe and examined it again.

Now, a peculiar tingling spread over Callista's body. She snatched the recipe from Tom's hand, and it suddenly made sense to her. It was as if the letters all came together in the right order, and she could make them out clearly. But from what she read, the process of actually brewing the elixir wouldn't be easy.

It took them three whole days of painstakingly measuring and heating the ingredients. The timings and amounts of ingredients were so specific that they didn't dare deviate from the instructions. The last ingredient to go in was a single drop of Callista's blood.

Eventually, their concoction was complete.

Callista held up the vial of deep golden liquid, complete

with floating slivers of shining blue that flitted in and out of sight as the mixture was shaken.

"Should I drink it?" Callista's voice was suddenly hoarse and dry. She coughed in an attempt to clear the dryness that seemed to have come from nowhere.

Tom looked carefully at the mixture. "It's up to you, Callista. But think about it carefully before you do. If all this is true, and it really will give you eternal youth, you are tying yourself to a lifetime of this war. It said in the recipe that you will never age but will spend forever fighting the Brotherhood. If you don't take it, you're turning your back on the war and your people but you could live a normal, mortal life."

Callista sighed. "I don't think I could lead a normal life. If Yvonne has taken the elixir to the Brotherhood, then they'll be coming for us. It sounds like this war is part of my destiny. I don't think I'll escape it wherever I go. Taking this may be the only thing that keeps us alive."

Tom said nothing in response but gave a sad smile.

Callista paced again, talking to herself more than to Tom. "I've got a responsibility here. All of those people are waiting for me to return as their leader. Wouldn't it be better to return with some sort of power? A promise of eternal youth? I can give it to everyone, and they'll all stay young forever. We can train together and get better and better. Good enough to defeat the Brotherhood."

She had made her decision. Callista yanked the stopper from the top of the bottle. With a deep breath and a nagging voice telling her she could never go back once she did this, she tipped her head back and took a deep swig from the vial.

The delicious golden liquid flowed down her throat, instantly warming her throughout. Within seconds of the elixir entering her stomach, she felt stronger, healthier, as if it had fortified her entire system. The recipe had said that even a quarter of the mixture would have the desired effects, so Callista made sure only to drink as much as she needed.

Something in the potion gave Callista new vigour and a determination to do what was right by her people. She couldn't know if it had truly given her eternal youth. She would have to wait years to be sure of that. But it had certainly invigorated her.

"Here's what we'll do," she said, addressing Tom. "We should take as much of this back with us as we can. If there isn't enough, we'll come back for more, but I want every single person back at that camp to have this. Not just the Children of Light supporters outside the temple but everybody back at the survivor camp as well."

Tom nodded slowly, but seemed sceptical. "Everyone? Are you sure?"

There was no doubt in Callista's mind. "Yes, of course. They're lost and in mourning. If I return with this, it will give them something to live for."

"But if everybody takes it, there will be immortals walking the planet and using their eternal youth to do whatever they like. What if they start abusing it? Can you trust each of those people, strangers, to treat the elixir with respect, to understand the responsibility that comes with eternal youth?"

Tom's argument was based on logic. Callista could see his point, but it made her uncomfortable. How could she justify having something like this in her hands and not give it to everybody?

"Even if they don't understand the responsibility, surely they still deserve a chance, don't they? Isn't it up to them to do what they want with their lives, whether they're immortal or not?"

"Of course, but we need these people. You said they're going to be your army. That's what the Book told you to do, right? Set up an army? Then we need those people with us. Besides, it just took us days to brew one vial. We can't keep on making them for just anybody. Only certain people should have it."

"How can I break it to those people that only some can take the elixir?"

"Simple. Offer them a choice. They can only take it if they pledge themselves to you and your cause."

Callista thought about it and nodded slowly. It did seem to be the most logical solution. She picked up the vial, fixed Tom in a serious stare and said, "If I can only give this to my army, will you stand by me and fight?"

He threw his head back and laughed. "Your army! I'd never have believed that!"

She nudged him playfully with her elbow. "So, will you take it? Will you join me?"

He smirked and took the vial from her. Without a moment's hesitation, he yanked the stopper from the top and guzzled the entire thing in one huge gulp. His eyes widened, and his skin seemed to glow. He tossed the vial over his shoulder and, ignoring the smash behind him, grabbed Callista's waist with both hands, pulling her towards him with a kiss.

She glowed inside, feeling his warm hands on her hips and his lips upon hers. "You didn't even need to ask, Callista. Of course, I'll follow you. I'll follow you anywhere. And there's no way you're getting into a fight without me to back you up."

She slapped him playfully again, but her expression became more serious. "Thank you, Tom. I needed to know you were here beside me."

Tom reached up and brushed a strand of golden hair from her eyes. "There should never have been any doubt."

Callista, relieved, sank into his arms and rested her head

against his chest, trying to comprehend the enormity of what lay ahead. She knew what she had to do. From here on, her life would never be the same again. The carefree teenager who spent her time lazily hanging around with her friends or practising martial arts with the boy she had a crush on was gone. The desperation and revelation of the past few days had aged her considerably, and now an adult's head rested upon her young shoulders.

"This is it. We take the Book and as much of this elixir as we can brew and carry, and we'll head back to the camp."

"Will they believe us?" Tom asked.

She released a heavy sigh. "We can only try. If we show them the Book and explain how we felt when we drank the potion, that's the best we can do. If they choose not to believe, that's their decision. If they don't pledge their loyalty to our cause, they don't take it. It's as simple as that."

CHAPTER FOURTEEN

Callista and Tom spent the next week brewing as much of the elixir as they could. It took considerably less time than the first mixing, now that they knew what to do. After some experimentation, they discovered that only a tiny shaving of time fragment was needed for each one, and Callista was relieved that the supplies she had gathered would last a long time.

When they felt they had enough, Tom and Callista took the batches of elixir back to the villagers.

Busy with wood carving, food gathering and weaving, the people took a few moments to notice that Callista had reappeared. When they saw her, they froze, their eyes fixed on *The Book of Alcherys* in her left hand and the glass vial of elixir in her right.

There were audible gasps of surprise, before some of the older members dropped to their knees, wringing their hands and wiping at the tears in their eyes. Callista was humbled by their treatment of her. For the first time, she began to feel like the ruler she was supposed to become. Holding the two most sacred objects to this ancient civilisation in her young hands, she felt not just like a leader but a god.

They gathered around her as she held the Book and elixir up for them all to see. They murmured to one another, unable to believe their eyes, but when she began to speak, they dropped silent immediately.

"Descendants of the Children of Light, you have lived by the rules and traditions of this noble way of life for many years. I am a novice, but I know that you will support me and stand by my side as we learn together how best to survive, to grow and to reclaim the planet from those who seek to destroy it." The words came naturally to her. She didn't need to think of what to say as something deep within her awakened, and the spirits of her ancestors spoke through her.

"I hold here, in my hands, the fabled and long-hidden relics from the great era that came before this one. *The Book of Alcherys—*" There was a collective gasp of awe from the people gathered before her, "—has taught me the ways of my ancestors. I intend to walk in their footsteps and guide our people back to former glory. To do that, I have brewed a tonic of eternal youth, the elixir."

More gasps of shock rippled around the gathering. "A few sips of this will halt the ageing process and allow you to remain forever young. However, to be afforded this privilege, you must swear your undying loyalty to our cause. You must be willing to give up your time, your dedication and even your lives to ensure the ways of our people survive. Who will join me in an eternal quest against the Brotherhood?"

She hadn't needed to ask. Every single member of the camp wholeheartedly pledged their support to Callista and the Children of Light. Within an hour, they had all taken the elixir. Callista looked proudly upon the beginnings of her army and knew that this was what she had been born to do. This was truly in her blood, and in her soul.

"You did it, Callista," Tom said, joining her and interlocking his fingers with hers. "You have your army, and you even have a guidebook to help you rule." He nodded to *The Book of Alcherys*, which she had placed on a table at the side of the camp. "Now we need to train the people and prepare them for whatever lies ahead."

But Callista frowned. "No, I don't think we're done yet. The survivor camp. I want to go back and bring the survivors into our army."

"Really?" Tom was sceptical. "These people here are believers, loyal to a fault, and they are willing to live and die for you. Those at the camp are random stragglers. They could cause trouble, question your authority, break the rules."

"I know, Tom. I know all of that, but one of the hallmarks of my new leadership is to look out for the peoples of the world, all of them. I couldn't justify being a leader and allowing those who don't fit in to just die."

"You don't know they'd die. They could do just fine."

"No. I can't do it. They might survive, yes, or they might die of disease or injury. They might be slaughtered by the Brotherhood. If the Brotherhood comes looking for me, they might track me to the camp, and I can't leave those people in danger. It isn't fair."

"You can't save everybody."

"I know that, but I can help those that are left. It would only be a few days out of my way, and if they agree to join us, we could double the size of the army." Tom still looked at her like she was insane. "There are kids there, Tom."

Heaving a deep sigh, Tom smiled at her. "You're the boss."

* * *

When the early morning sun had risen above the horizon, and the world was bathed in a comforting orange glow, they set out. Their pockets and hands were full of bottles of elixir. Callista's head was in turmoil for the first part of the long walk back to the camp. What if they laughed and brushed her off as crazy and deluded?

How could she convince anybody that a mere teenager was so crucial to this war? What if they didn't even believe that a war was going to happen?

Laughing at her was the least of her problems. What if they ganged up together and attacked her and Tom to get the elixir? She shuddered and shook her head to clear the dark and terrifying thoughts from her mind.

The second part of the journey was easier. Exhaustion made Callista's limbs heavy, and with that numbness in her body came a fuzziness in her head. All the negativity was, if not entirely dismissed, pushed to the back of Callista's mind. She shouldn't worry about the other survivors attacking her. Tom was there to help. And if they laughed, so be it. They wouldn't be laughing when the Brotherhood armies arrived and the horrible prophecies of demons and the dead came to pass. She could worry about these things forever, but it wouldn't do anybody any good. She had to keep her head straight for when she saw her people. Even if they seemed rude or aggressive, at the core of it all, she knew they were scared. What they needed was a strong leader, and Callista hoped she could be that for them.

The sun was beginning to drop lower in the evening sky when they passed over the last hill, and the encampment came into view. Tom let out a loud whoop of joy and gathered Callista in his arms.

"I didn't want to say, but I kind of thought we were lost. It seemed far longer on the way back than on the way out there."

Callista slapped him playfully.

Tom grinned in response and kissed her on the cheek before they continued on the last part of their journey. Exclamations of relief and surprise rang out through the camp as they saw Callista and Tom approach. A few of the more prominent members of the group ventured out to meet them. They introduced themselves as Mark and Rick and then dived straight into the questions.

"What did you find out there? Are there other survivors?"

Callista smiled at the two men in an attempt to reassure them. "Let's get everyone together around the central fire, and I'll fill you in on everything."

Mark and Rick nodded and dashed off to gather everybody.

Callista's heart was hammering in her chest, her fingers jittering nervously until Tom gently wrapped his comforting hands around hers. "Just tell them the truth. Everything will fall into place, I'm sure of it."

The doubts that had wracked her mind drifted away at Tom's calm, reassuring words. She gave a determined nod and jumped up onto the log she had used before to address the survivors. They gathered around her, some sitting cross-legged on the ground, others perched on rocks or logs, still more standing at the back, with questioning glances or concerned frowns.

Callista took a deep breath and began. "Tom and I have returned from the ruins of an ancient city. What we found there has shocked me, but at the same time it all makes sense."

She gripped *The Book of Alcherys* tightly in her hand and held it aloft so all could see. "I found this book. It explains what happened in the past, long before this tragic event. It knew the oceans would rise and the fire would fall. It also knows about us. There is a section in this book, written hundreds of years ago, that speaks of a group of people that will survive this apocalypse, who will band together and fight against the forces of evil that caused it. I believe with every bone in my body that we are that group. If the book was right about everything else, why shouldn't it be right about this?"

"So why did this happen?" Mark called out, his face screwed up in scepticism.

Callista took another deep breath to calm her nerves and looked over to Tom, who gave her a reassuring nod. "I don't know how it happened, but I believe that some force higher than us did it deliberately. It intended to wipe the world clean of those it didn't want or need. We few survivors are the ones who are left to inherit the planet."

There were snorts of derision and disbelief. Some people even rose to their feet, shaking their heads.

"Hey!" Callista called out. Everybody stopped walking away to look at her. "You may not believe me, and that's fine. I don't expect you to trust some random book we found in some ruins. If you want to take your chances with the world out there, be my guest, but I truly believe that the only way we can survive is if we all stick together. A war is coming. That is inevitable. This apocalypse was clearing the planet of people to make our planet one huge battleground for the war that will ravage our lands."

Silence descended on the group as people stared blankly at the ground or cast frightened eyes at the woods and fields around them as if expecting dangers to pop out from behind every bush.

"I know you're frightened. Hell, I'm frightened too. If what this book says is true, our enemies, the ones who will be coming for us any day, have been preparing for this for years. They won't be afraid. They will be marching towards us with their heads held high, and their swords sharp for the kill. They are called the Brotherhood of Shadow, and they will decimate all they come across. They will maim and kill. Nothing is sacred in their world, because they cling to an ideology that demands the death of everybody other than their followers."

There were panicked whispers and frightened looks on the faces of all who sat before her. Callista cursed herself for being so blunt. She jumped down from the log and walked up to each of them in turn, trying to establish a connection as she spoke.

"I'm not saying this to frighten you. The war has not yet begun. We have time if we act now. And we have some significant advantages that will improve life for us all. I found many things in those ruins, not just the Book. I also found money, huge piles of money. We can start our own economy, trade with other survivors, if there are any out there. And I bet that if we think hard enough, each of us has skills we can use to help our new society. We can set up camp here, make this place our home. Every one of us is needed to make it work. You are all special. You are all a crucial part of what we hope to achieve."

Even those who had been sceptical before now hung off Callista's every word as she glowed with authority.

"And when the war comes, we will need soldiers. We will need men and women who are willing to lay their lives on the line to protect our new nation. It's a dangerous job, but there is an incentive. In those ruins, I found this." She took a vial of elixir from Tom and held it high for all to see. "This is the Elixir of Light, a tonic that provides eternal youth to the drinker. It is safe, and I am confident that it works. Tom and I already drank it, and I can feel the effects buzzing in my veins."

Every pair of eyes locked onto the glass vial as Callista paraded backwards and forwards.

"But it is not to be taken lightly. Drinking this doesn't mean you'll live forever. Drinking this," she held it high again to emphasise her point, "ties you to an eternity fighting for our people. It means you cannot leave us, it means your fate is tied to ours. When the armies come, you are expected to fight."

The survivors were stunned and stared at her in silence. Some cast their eyes away from the elixir, fearful of its great power, while others stared hungrily at it, desperate for just a drop.

"Who amongst you would be brave enough to fight, even when it looks futile, even when the future is cloudy, and our fate seems doomed?"

For a few moments, there was only silence, occasionally broken by a hurried mumbling, or a whispered comment to a neighbour. Eventually, Mark and Rick stepped forwards, side by side. Mark held his head high and faced Callista.

"If what you say is true and war really is coming, then I want to fight. I don't want to stand by and let these people be killed. I want to do something about it."

"And you, Rick?"

"Me too."

Callista was almost overwhelmed with gratitude. Ignoring the urge to leap forwards and hug the strangers, she nodded serenely and held out the vial of elixir. The two men stared at the bottle with wide eyes, looking both intrigued and afraid.

Callista hesitated before handing it over. "I need you both to understand what this means. This is not a gift or reward. It needs to be a symbol of your dedication to this group of people. Once you drink it, you are handing your lives over to protect our new society, forever. It won't make you immortal. You'll still be able to die through illness or injury. It will just stop you from ageing. Remember to use this eternal youth to start afresh in life, to leave everything from your past lives behind and begin again, reborn as guardians of our people."

Rick and Mark glanced at each other, then back to Callista. They both nodded. Callista smiled in relief and gratitude. She handed them the vial. Both young men stared intently as if mentally preparing themselves for the enormity of what they were about to do.

"Wait," Mark said quietly. "I want to do this the right way. I don't want to be the old me anymore. Everything that made me 'Mark' has gone, and all of the people who called me by that name are missing or dead. If this is a new start, then I want to be known by a new name."

Callista nodded. "I like the idea of that. Total rebirth into a new life. What name do you want to go by?"

"I have no idea."

"Well, what were you interested in before all this happened? What did you want to be?"

"It's stupid...but I loved space. It was my dream to study Mars."

"Mars!" Callista said, her eyes lighting up with delight. "That's perfect. It's not even too different to Mark!"

A smile crept across Mark's face, and Callista saw proper joy in him for the first time. "Mars it is," he said and, taking the first swig of elixir. He gasped for air as the peculiar liquid ran down his throat. Callista patted him on the back and gave him a huge smile as the others gathered around and erupted into a cheer. She took the vial back from him and handed the rest to Rick.

"How about you? Do you want a completely new start?"

He nodded. "I do. I really do. I've always believed that our lives are mapped out for us by the stars. So, somebody or something wanted me to do this, to survive and take this elixir. I feel like I've been guided by the stars, so I'll go with my star sign. I'll be Aries."

More cheers and claps as he drank. It was all coming together.

"Callista!" She spun around to see Tom. He took her hands

and looked deep into her eyes. "What these guys did has inspired me. I want a new start too. Would you be offended if I changed my name?"

Callista laughed. "Of course not!"

"OK. I really feel that what Rick—Sorry, Aries—said about fate was true. So, I'll go with my star sign too. From now on, I'll be Scorpio."

Just hearing that simple word "Scorpio" made Callista's heart jump into her throat. Seven innocuous letters which had caused her pain just days ago now made her soul dance with joy. First love, loyal husband, a dedicated soldier to stay by her side, Callista had read all about the legendary Scorpio in *The Book of Alcherys*.

"What's up with you?" Tom asked, looking at Callista's open-mouthed stare.

She closed her mouth and forced it into a grin. "Nothing at all," she said. She threw herself into his arms, her lips locking fervently with his. He responded with passion, his warm embrace tightening around her, stroking her long golden hair.

"Hate to break this up and everything," Mars's voice broke into their oblivious little balloon, "but what do we do now? You said we're at war, right? Well, who with? What's this really about?"

Callista pulled away from Tom's arms, ran her hands over her face to compose herself, then stepped back up onto the fallen log that had become her pedestal.

"I know all of this is hard to take in, especially following the events of the past few days. But it has to be now. We cannot afford to wait. There was a battle which raged for centuries, two ancient societies at war. That war has begun to spill over into modern times, our world, our lives. It affects each and every one of us, or it will soon. It is my destiny to lead you. This responsibility has been dormant in my veins all of my life, and I never even knew it. But I know it now, and you are all here, ready to start a new life, protected by those of us who have agreed to give our lives to serve you."

She pointed to Tom, now Scorpio, Mars and Aries, who stood proudly with their heads high, then continued. "This very spot is where our new civilisation will begin. No, not a new civilisation, but a continuation of an ancient one. You are taking your place amongst history. Despite everything we have endured we, the last survivors, will prosper once more. Everybody will chip in, and if we don't have the skills already, we'll learn them."

Callista felt invincible, like her true purpose in life had finally been revealed to her.

"But what about this enemy you spoke of? The Brotherhood," cried a young woman with a small child clutching her leg.

"Yes, the Brotherhood of Shadow. They have been around for all of history, hidden, never quite within the public eye but waiting for their chance to rise up and take control of the world."

"Did they do this?" Aries asked quietly.

"No. I don't know who or what did this. I don't even know if it was planned or whether all of this is natural, but now the world has been wiped clean, the Brotherhood will take the opportunity to make this new world their own. I urge you all to read *The Book of Alcherys*. It explains everything and is important for our new society. It tells not only of the past but also of the future. It will instruct us in how to continue, what to watch out for and what pitfalls await us."

"A book? We're supposed to put our faith in some dusty old book you found?" A middle-aged man crossed his arms over his chest with a sceptical look in his eyes.

"I trust in it. I have never been a superstitious person, but when I read the wisdom written in those pages, it changed me. There are things in there that nobody could ever have known, things that were written hundreds of years ago. How can you explain that? It must have been written by somebody or something far bigger than any of us."

There was a wave of mutterings and sceptical head shaking. "Do you mean God?" a middle-aged man asked.

Callista shrugged. "I don't know exactly what I mean, but God or not, it is certainly something greater than us. And it has given us a path to survival, a comprehensive guide for how to get through all of this and ensure that humankind does not wither and die. Now we can either have faith and follow what it tells us, or we can throw it aside and go it alone. What do you think?"

Silence spread across the group, people either staring at Callista or avoiding eye contact altogether, but nobody argued with her. She took their silence as compliance and moved on to more positive things.

"From here on we can follow the Book, develop our new world exactly as we want it and build a nation we can be proud of. We will welcome new travellers or other survivors who have nowhere to go, but we must always be on the lookout for the Brotherhood of Shadow. After all, we are the only people on the planet left to oppose them. We are the Children of Light."

The clapping began, and finally cheers and whoops of delight. Before long, the whole settlement, all two hundred survivors, were clapping and cheering for Callista. She had never felt so strong. Looking at the faces of the people calling her name, invigorated by her words, told Callista the Book was right. She was a leader and always had been. She had just never known it.

Callista capitalised on her new confidence boost. She opened the Book to an image of a shield, split into eight sections. It was the same pattern as had been on the jigsaw in the first trial. She held it high for everybody to see. "This shield shows the eight nations, or armies, that will soon come to rule the world. We are one of these groups, a force to be reckoned with. From here on, this will be our symbol, to represent all that we are and all that we shall be."

She pointed to the symbol of the four daggers and the knot of infinity.

"For the rest of eternity, we will be strong. We have been given a chance, us and only us. We are special. We are chosen. Our destiny is written in our blood and in our souls. We will live, and we will grow at the heart of our new lands. We will call this place Alcherys, in honour of the nation that lay here before. No more will our kind be crushed by disaster, destroyed on the whim of unknown beings. We are here, and we shall stand tall forevermore!"

Any words that Callista spoke after that were swept away in the roar of adulation that followed. She jumped down and faced Scorpio, who gave her a restrained smile with a new admiration in his eyes.

Their partnership at the helm was about to begin.

EPILOGUE

Twigs and branches littered the forest floor. Yvonne stepped over them carefully, trying to avoid making too much noise. She walked for hours, increasing the distance between herself and the new Children of Light encampment. Eventually, she stopped, in the centre of the forest.

Taking a deep breath, she shuddered from head to toe, and the skin of her fingers began peeling back like the skin of a banana. It flopped, empty and lifeless, as the true form beneath broke free. Smoky plumes of darkness billowed where her human fingers had been just moments ago. As the skin peeled back further, her true self emerged, stepping out of the loose human covering and casting it aside.

'Yvonne' had fulfilled her purpose, and the Bavelize stood in her place. Thick, grey smoke, writhing and undulating, free of form, yet gathered together in the vague shape of a human being. The creature waved its smoky hands, weaving and pulling at invisible strands in the air, prying them apart to create a slit in the air. Pulling and wrenching at the crack, it tore a hole in the fabric of the dimension and stepped through, closing the hole tightly behind it with another wave of its hand.

Fire. Sulphur. Searing heat and burning flesh. If the creature had skin, it would have burnt right from its skeleton. But as an ethereal being, made of a higher substance, the heat and flames made no impact upon it.

Within seconds of it being in the realm of Hell, a figure appeared, large, imposing, and terrifying to gaze upon. It was an immense hulking monster, made of bizarre angles and jutting bone, with spikes and edges all over its body. It would have looked like a jagged bed of rocks were it not for the bright colours splashed across it. Oranges, reds and yellows, garish and startling, covered the creature, and nestled into its face were two glowing red slits for eyes.

"Bavelize. Good to see you." Its voice was deep and thunderous, booming and echoing across the fiery landscape.

The Bavelize nodded its featureless head, smoke swirling and writhing where its eyes should have been. It wasted no time with pleasantries.

"Thanatos. It has begun. The plan is underway." The Bavelize's words echoed, coming from everywhere and nowhere at once.

Thanatos grinned maniacally, his eyes glowing with red embers. "Then you have found the Dual Leaders?"

"Yes." The word hung in the air like mist, "They are equal. Perfectly equal. I've waited for many years in the hope of getting two leaders who are worthy of their titles, who can lead their nations to war. Neither will be able to defeat the other. They are both too strong. And both armies are immortal now. I've made sure of that. They will grow in power over the centuries until it is impossible for them to develop any further, and then it will be time."

Thanatos tilted his head to one side, looking at the Bavelize quizzically. "Then it would seem that my demons' involvement in your little apocalypse has enabled you to get to this point?"

The silence was palpable, hanging stagnant around them. Eventually, the Bavelize spoke. "Yes."

"Then I trust our deal stands? In centuries' time, when the war reaches its climax, our realm will be left untouched." Thanatos stared at the Bavelize, trying to work out where its eyes should have been.

"That was the deal, and I shall honour it. But I will require the demons' services again, I am sure."

Thanatos threw his head back in a booming laugh. "And we will be more than glad to assist. My demons long for a chance to walk the Human Realm again."

"They'll be released when we have need of them. The people aren't strong enough yet to handle their presence, but in a hundred years or more, the armies will be strong enough to cope with their threat."

Thanatos nodded, accepting the deal as reasonable. "So, where will you go to oversee the war? Will you take a disguise again?"

"There is no need to hide behind a disguise for now. I will continue to lead the Brotherhood of Shadow. They need my guidance more. When I show my true form, their leader will be frightened into submission. He will follow my every word. The Brotherhood are superstitious, and have hung onto their traditions and beliefs for years. They need a god more than anything. The Children of Light are just babies. I don't want to scare them, but I may appear to them in disguise from time to time to guide their way."

Thanatos laughed. "A great plan. But what happens if one of the armies becomes stronger than the other? What happens if one leader kills the other before you are ready?"

"That will never happen. I'll make sure of it." With those final words, the Bavelize dissipated in a swirl of smoky tendrils and plumes, on its way to the Brotherhood of Shadow.

Read on for a teaser preview of the next novella in The Light and Shadow Chronicles: Origin of Shadow. *This novella complements* Genesis of Light *and gives the origin of the Brotherhood of Shadow.*

PREVIEW—ORIGIN OF SHADOW

The ticking of the clock was far louder than it should have been. Every innocuous click of the hands seemed to reverberate around the room, intensifying the tension that hung in the air. Vincent Wilder stood perfectly still, making sure his chin was raised and his expression stony. He tried to hide the fact that his fingers twitched nervously behind his back. He had to concentrate. He had to ensure that this went off without a hitch. He made an effort to narrow his eyes and puff out his chest, hoping his frame was imposing, threatening even.

A single drop of sweat trickled its way down his forehead, running a sticky trail down his skin. He wanted to reach up and wipe it away but didn't dare draw attention to the fact that he was perspiring. Sure, it meant he was hot, but would they take it as a sign of weakness? Would it be too obvious that he was nervous? So, he did nothing, and let the salty drop work its way down his forehead and into his dark eyes. He blinked to clear the drop, but his vision merely blurred and itched. He could hold off no longer and was forced to swipe at his eyes with a hurried hand.

His eyesight cleared and he took the opportunity to glance down at the table before him and the people sat around it. A couple in their early forties sat on one side of the small metal table, close together, huddling for comfort. But their eyes were strong and defiant, the woman's in particular. Her hands were flat on the table top and she spoke with determination, leaning forwards, as if to stress the importance of her words.

The man beside her was silent and although a stony expression was plastered across his face, Vincent was sure he could see the man's hands trembling.

Across from them sat Franco Wilder, Vincent's father. Once, he had had a thick shock of dark hair, long and wild, draped across his shoulders. That was how Vincent always saw his father in his mind, but the figure that sat before him had changed drastically in the past few years. Once Franco's hair had started thinning, he had shaved the lot, and the bald head somehow made the most terrifying man Vincent had ever met even more intimidating.

Franco's posture was rigid and unmoving, a coiled snake waiting to lunge. The dark eyes that had silently chastised Vincent since childhood were now solidly locked onto the couple before him. His father's fingers were locked together tightly, but Vincent knew that it would only take a split-second for him to wrench the knife from its concealed pouch on his thigh. Vincent's muscles were primed, tightened and ready to leap into a fight. He had learnt never to relax around his father. It was dangerous and foolish, and the threat of violence was never far away.

"Tomorrow evening? No," Franco's voice was unwavering. Many a customer would have wilted under his fierce glare, but the woman held her shoulders high and straightened her back.

"Then you don't really want my business. It was a pleasure dealing with you, Mister Wilder." She started to stand up, brushing down her fitted grey suit.

"Wait. Mrs. Nienna, Mr. Nienna. I'm sure we can arrive at some sort of agreement." Vincent balked a little at seeing his father cowering before such lowly figures, but he was intrigued by what game his dad was playing.

The outwardly calm demeanour his father expressed would have been convincing to many, but it didn't fool Vincent.

He saw the way his dad's fingers drummed the surface of the table. He saw the unnaturally tense shoulders in a man who was usually in control of every situation. He wasn't the only one to see the effect the couple were having on Franco either. The woman hadn't sat back down yet and stood tall over Franco, trying to dominate him with her presence.

Shivers ran down Vincent's spine. He bristled with the desire to teach her a lesson, to punish her for daring to condescend to the greatest man he had ever known.

"I want two kilos of Sarro, and I'll pay eight thousand. But it has to be tomorrow. I need to make sure I catch the boats if I want maximum distribution. And how will anybody in Pabell get a taste for Wilder Sarro if the taverns and docks run dry?" The woman snapped, cool and calculated.

With a polite smile on his face and his head tilted slightly to the side, Franco considered her offer, but Vincent saw the darkness in his dad's eyes. His father had absolutely no intention of accepting the drug deal, and Vincent would have staked his entire savings on the fact.

"Of course, I would normally gut anybody even suggesting such an insult to our family name. Eight thousand is a pittance for such a quantity of the strongest intoxicant on the market." Franco sat forwards, his fingers intertwined, chin resting upon his tented hands. Vincent tensed, preparing to support his father, hands tensing upon the knife he had hidden behind his back.

The tattoo at the back of Franco's neck twitched, the black phoenix etched there stretching its wings as Franco tilted his head from side to side.

"But just this once, I can make an exception. As you say, they need to get a taste for it, right?"

Vincent broke his vow of silence as he nearly staggered forwards with the shock. "Father?"

Franco's head snapped around to look at his son and his face was filled with pure disgust and anger. Vincent nodded in deference and forced himself back to his guard position behind his father.

"Tomorrow evening. At the docks. I bring my men, you bring yours and we make the exchange," Franco said quietly. "It'll be a strain to get so much harvested and purified in time, but you leave me no option."

"I trust the quality will not suffer?"

Franco stiffened in annoyance. "Don't worry. Every kid with a spare pocketful of coins will be dribbling and retching in a backstreet gambling den or tavern before you know it."

Mrs. Nienna nodded firmly, and the man at her side visibly relaxed. Franco rose from his seat to match her height, and they were back on a level playing field again. It was a strange sight to behold, a slight woman squaring off against one of the most notorious barons in the city. But something wasn't right. Vincent was sure of that, but he couldn't put his finger on the problem.

"Karla—if I may call you that—allow me to check the terms of our arrangement. We will bring two kilograms of pure Sarro. No additives, no preservatives." He paused and stared at her. "Unmarked, opaque wrapping."

Her mouth broke into a sly smile. "And we will bring our eight thousand."

A slight nod of the head was the only reply that Franco gave. Vincent shifted uncomfortably from one foot to the other, his mind reeling as he struggled to work out why his father would accept such a deal. He usually demanded far higher prices for the same product.

"Then it seems that our business is concluded, Mr. Wilder," Mrs. Nienna said as she rose to her feet. The man stood beside her, his eyes intense and serious, but still he said nothing. His shoulders were tensed, like the hackles of a cat, and Vincent could see the distrust in his face. They shook hands. Vincent stood his ground, even though every muscle in his body was screaming to leap to his father's side. He didn't trust these people one bit. There was something different about them, unusual. He had dealt with common thieves and bandits all his life. When he had left school at fourteen, he had grown up with them, drank with them, and fought beside them. These people didn't look like the usual pickpockets or narcotic pushers, and they didn't sound like them either. None of it made any sense.

Only when the door closed behind them did Franco step up beside his son, bulky arms crossed over his chest, which was beginning to thicken in his later years.

"Go on. Ask me," Franco said quietly.

"Why did you accept such a bad deal? I don't understand."

Franco stared at the closed door, his jaw chewing as though he had gum in his mouth. Pretending he was busy chewing something often bought him precious seconds of extra thinking time in tense negotiations. It was a tactic that Vincent admired, but in the heat of a tense deal with local thugs or armed outlaws he never remembered such things himself. His mind was busy turning at a hundred miles an hour as it was.

"Come on, son. Think about it."

Vincent frowned as he ran back over the details of the meeting. "It doesn't make any sense. You never accept less than twelve thousand for that amount of Sarro. They said they're pushing it to the marketplaces and taverns, but who'd buy from them? Everybody knows we run the Sarro trade around here. Nobody would dare buy from them. It's almost as if..."

Franco turned to him, arms still crossed, jaw incessantly gnawing. "Say it."

"It's almost as if it wasn't a real deal." Vincent's words

drifted off into oblivion as the realisation came to him. "They aren't used to buying, are they? They haven't done it before, or...they're not even genuine customers."

The side of Franco's mouth twitched in an acknowledging click.

"That's why you agreed to such a fleecing. You knew it wouldn't go through anyway."

A nod of the head confirmed Vincent's suspicions.

"So, who are they? And why follow it through if you knew it was all a fake?"

"I wanted to meet them, to see if they truly are who I thought."

"And, who do you think they are?"

Franco's face broke into a rarely-seen grin. It was almost grotesque. "They are our enemies. The ones who are trying to bring us down."

ABOUT THE AUTHOR

D.M. Cain is a dystopian and fantasy author working for . The Light and Shadow Chronicles series features a range of books which can be read in any order. Series instalments include and . D.M. Cain is working on the next novel in the Light and Shadow Chronicles series, *The Sins of Silas*, as well as another complementary novella entitled *Origin of Shadow*.

Cain has released one stand-alone novel: , a psychological thriller set in a dystopian future. The Phoenix Project was the winner of the 2016 Kindle Book Review Best Sci-Fi novel Award.

D.M. Cain is also a member of the International Thriller Writers and one of the creators and administrators of the online author group #Awethors. Her short story *The End* was published in : *an anthology by the #Awethors*.

Cain lives in Leicestershire, UK with her two young children, and spends her time reading, writing, reviewing and indulging in geek culture (Marvel, Game of Thrones, Star Wars, Harry Potter, Final Fantasy).

Connect with D.M. Cain at

Facebook profile: DM Cain

Twitter: @DMCain84

Thank you for buying this book. Independent and small press authors do all marketing and promoting of their books themselves; therefore, if you enjoyed this book, please leave a review with your retailer of choice. I would be most grateful for your support. Thank you.

For background information, character profiles, extra content and sneak peeks at upcoming books in the series, visit or sign up for my mailing list here: .

Genesis Of Light
ISBN: 978-4-86750-055-2

Published by
Next Chapter
1-60-20 Minami-Otsuka
170-0005 Toshima-Ku, Tokyo
+818035793528

3rd June 2021

CPSIA information can be obtained
at www.ICGtesting.com
Printed in the USA
LVHW112302190721
693163LV00001B/111